When Lucy ran away from Max McGraw she had really been running away from Ted, the husband who had made her so unhappy. Now Max had found her again. Could she convince him he was wasting his time—or would *he* convince her that he could make her happy?

PACIFIC DISTURBANCE

BY

VANESSA GRANT

MILLS & BOON LIMITED
15–16 BROOK'S MEWS
LONDON W1A 1DR

First published in Great Britain 1985
by Mills & Boon Limited

This edition 1985

ISBN 0 263 75171 6

Set in Monophoto Plantin 11 on 11½ pt.
05–0885 – 49002

Made and printed in Great Britain by
Richard Clay (The Chaucer Press) Ltd,
Bungay, Suffolk

CHAPTER ONE

THE spring winds had been blowing all day, whipping the waters of the harbour into ever increasing turbulence. Adventurous amateur fishermen had long since given up trying to catch the record salmon. Just outside Prince Rupert harbour, three white salmon trawlers were moving slowly along the shoreline. Unlike the smaller boats, they were outfitted with stabilisers to control their rolling in the rough water.

Moments earlier, the Coast Guard radio operator had broadcast an updated Environment Canada forecast, predicting winds increasing to gale force on the north coast of British Columbia.

The fishermen had seen the sailing boat appear from the north; first as a white spot on the horizon, later as a large blue ketch carrying two sails. As the gusts whipped wild white water, the trawlers rolled despite the stabilising outriggers hanging from each side. The sailing boat, wind howling along her sails, pushed hard through the water.

On board *Wanderlust*, Max McGraw was nestled securely in the cockpit corner, one hand on the wheel, an unruly, wind-tossed lock of hair escaping the hood of his cruiser suit. In the opposite corner was David, his twelve-year-old son. Under Max, *Wanderlust*'s motion assured him that she was carrying her sails well, glorying in the gale as an opportunity to do what she was built to do. An hour ago Max had reduced sail in the face of the strengthening wind. Since that time, the gusts had continued to strengthen, and he was considering reducing sail again.

Wanderlust rode down the side of a wave to meet the upcoming surge. Water rushed loudly against the starboard hull as she pushed down, then lifted with the upcoming wave. Max welcomed the feel of the wind whipping against his face. A large wave broke over the bow to send green water streaming along the decks. *Wanderlust* ploughed on through the seas, more than equal to the violence around her.

'We'll tack in a minute,' he shouted to his son. 'Then we'll come in behind the Kinahan Islands to anchor for the night. Take a look at the chart, see——' The noise of the wind drowned his final words.

David was excited, unwilling to go below. 'This is great! Do you think we'll get more wind? Is it going to last?'

'You're not going to miss it if you go down,' his father shouted back, smiling at the boy's unwillingness to leave the excitement. 'This storm is going to last at least until tomorrow.'

David closed the hatch behind himself as he disappeared below. Max watched him go thoughtfully. David had taken well to cruising life, was learning responsibilities and skills that would ease his path into manhood.

The joy of sailing the wild west coast of Canada with David had given Max a great deal of satisfaction in recent weeks; but neither his enjoyment of his son nor his love for this yacht could totally erase the emptiness that had become his constant companion.

The lines on his lean brown face deepened. The brown eyes grew sombre. He was deeply aware of his own loneliness; deeply aware that months of searching had brought him no hint of Lucy's whereabouts. His assumption—that she was still somewhere in Canada—was based on hope, not evidence. If she had left the country, he had no idea where to look for her.

A year ago, when Lucy disappeared, he had turned to work for forgetfulness. In work he had found only memories of Lucy. He had known he loved her almost from the first, but it was her leaving that had showed him the agonising depth of that love. She had become so much a part of his life that when she left, he could not sit down to a meal without seeing her across from him; could not work without remembering her ideas, her words, her face. His life had become a progression of memories . . . memories of how he had courted her carefully, sensing the wariness in her. Despite her caution, her avoidance of any personal commitments, he had seen her affection for him growing. Lucy hadn't revealed the mystery of her past to him, but increasingly she had been unable to keep herself from responding to the love Max felt for her until, finally, he had known the taste of victory—and love.

Short-lived victory. The following day she had disappeared.

After too many weeks of empty memories he realised that she was too deeply a part of him, that he must do whatever he could to find her again.

David climbed back into the cockpit with a cup of coffee for his father. The freshly-made coffee burned as Max swallowed the first aromatic mouthful.

'When will we get to Prince Rupert, Dad?' David had hot chocolate for himself. He warmed his hands on the cup, sipping carefully. He moved gently with the motion of the yacht to avoid spilling any of the hot liquid.

Another coastal town. Although she had never been willing to relax her guard enough to come sailing with Max, Lucy's eyes had always lit up at the sight of boats, at talk of sailing and the ocean. He had searched so many of these towns for her; he had little hope that this one would produce any sign of her. 'We'll be there tomorrow night,' he said.

When dark fell, *Wanderlust* was anchored in the vee formed by the two Kinahan Islands. The noise of wind was all around Max and David, but the water in their anchorage moved gently, away from the force of the storm.

When David was in bed, Max moved about the boat, tidying, listening to the new forecast on his radio. Finally, he sat quietly in the cockpit with a hot drink, watching the trees moving in the wind, the faint loom of Prince Rupert's light in the sky.

He saw Lucy's face clearly, animated with some idea from her quick mind. How many times had he watched her, listening, arguing some point with her? He saw her face soften, saw the stirrings of desire as he bent towards her, as he moved his hands through her soft auburn curls.

If he failed to find her, would her image in his mind ever dim?

Lucy's eyes were firmly fixed on the man in front

of her. His name was Terry Goodwin, and he was well into his tale of woe, describing his business problems to her. His worry emphasised a developing double chin. His sandy fair hair might have been turning to grey, but no one could be sure. Lucy suspected that his oddly-parted hair was combed to conceal a prematurely receding hairline.

If she concentrated hard, watching his lips move and hearing his words, she could tune out the party until she heard only Terry. Not that Terry was exciting, or even interesting; but he was a businessman and he might be a customer—that was enough reason to concentrate on him.

Someone turned up the music, and the large living room vibrated with modern music. The settler who had built this old Prince Rupert house in the early years of the century was probably turning in his grave. Lucy lost her hold on Terry Goodwin's conversation. Across the room, she could see John struggling through the crowd at the bar. He had two glasses in his hands and he was heading towards her now.

She wished she hadn't come. She could have stayed in the office and worked on a computer program. She could have gone for a walk on the waterfront. Either way, she would have avoided this crowd. She wasn't comfortable in crowds, and lately the sight of other couples dancing and playing the moves of love had only intensified her loneliness.

She had come only because John seemed to want it so much. John had been good company in the last few months, good conversation and no demands on her—at least not until recently.

Lately he had begun to act as if their relationship should be deeper; a development she found alarming.

As the music level diminished, she heard Terry making noises, wondering if her computer service might solve his business problems, worrying about getting involved in a technology he didn't understand.

She reassured him. She worked at concentrating on his worries until she once more forgot the party around her. Terry Goodwin was flattered. He thought there was something special about Lucy Carter. He would have described her as beautiful, but he would have been wrong. Her hair was beautiful, the curly auburn halo standing out among the other women. Something in her face marked her as a woman who had seen more, done more, than any of the others present. He was immensely flattered that she found his words interesting, that she was spending her time talking to him. He had a wife and five children at home, but for a few moments he felt a taste of adventure.

Lucy became aware of John at her side. She took the drink he held out, but didn't raise it to her lips; she was involved in communicating the basics of computer accounting to Terry. John touched her waist possessively with his hand and she was unaware of the touch at first. Later, when she realised his arm had settled possessively around her waist, she moved away.

'Shall we have something to eat, John? I'm starving!'

There was a buffet spread out in the next room and they piled their plates high, Terry still by their side, talking, working on holding Lucy's attention. John became silent and sulky, until Terry's wife appeared to claim her errant husband.

Later, in the car, Lucy realised he was angry. It was her fault for virtually ignoring her escort all evening. She valued John Fraser's friendship and she had no desire to see him angry and hurt. When he pulled up in front of her apartment building, she smiled at him. He saw it as a mysterious, elusive smile that made his arm tighten on her shoulder in case she should disappear.

'Coffee?' she offered, a peace-offering.

In her tiny kitchen, she seated him in a chair and bustled about with cupboards and an automatic filter coffee maker.

'Did you have a good time?' he asked.

'Yes, I did. I'm always nervous at parties—afraid I won't find anyone to talk to and will sit all evening being the outsider—but tonight was fun.' Except that she had had a strange feeling all evening; as if Max were there, watching her. Maybe that explained her poor manners in ignoring John, trying frantically to become involved in talk with Terry. She placed the coffee in front of him. He was looking critically at her apartment, giving suggestions for redecorating.

She concealed her resentment, knowing it was illogical of her to cling to the sterile, impersonal walls; to resist trading the dingy sofa for something brighter. 'I don't mind it,' she told him with a smile. 'It's only a place for me to live for a while. It doesn't matter. It's certainly not worth redecorating.' She hadn't worked on the apartment, hadn't been involved in anything but her business since leaving Toronto—since leaving Max. She looked around at her surroudings now, wondering if decorating would make any difference to how she felt; whether she would sleep better if the place felt more like a home.

John reached out to touch her shoulder. 'You can't work hard every day and come home alone. Tomorrow you must come to us—Mother would love to see you again. You can relax in a real home, put your feet up and let us look after you.'

She thought of a fireplace with warm wood walls reflecting a feeling of home. The image had more appeal than he could have known. All evening she had been conscious of her isolation, her loneliness. She suspected that John did not see the real Lucy when he looked at her; but she felt a desire to be the simple, uncomplicated creature he believed she was. Maybe his warm home could stir roots in her. Maybe this man . . .

Crazy! If she couldn't handle a relationship with Max, how could she succeed with any man? Years ago, Ted had spoiled all that for her. She was insane to think of a relationship with John; to think that his smooth, friendly good looks posed no threat to her peace. John was a pleasant man, not aggressive, not frightening. But if she let him kiss her—touch her—would not Ted's memory rise to torment her again?

When the coffee was gone, they moved into the living room. He suggested music, and she found a tape and pushed it into the stereo player. The music bathed her sterile apartment with a sentimental moodiness, and she closed her eyes. At her back she felt the comfortable, overstuffed sofa. The music worked its magic, until she imagined Max's lean, masculine frame beside her. The music twisted craftily in her mind with memories of Max's arms, Max's lips.

John lowered his lips to hers, probing gently for her response, and as he touched her, the fantasy dissolved. She forced herself to remain still in John's arms, analysing her response to the feel of him. His arms felt warm and secure and she willed her body to go soft as his hands moved gently over her back. She let her lips soften and open under his; she felt none of the passion that Max's hands had aroused in her, but no fear either.

John forgot about her skills, forgot that she was Lucy the elusive. In his arms she seemed soft and pliant—the very opposite to the aggressive, efficient young businesswoman she was by day.

His passion led him on. She felt his hands move to her breasts, caressing gently. She could feel the ice growing within herself as his hands firmed with desire. Panic surged inside her and she knew she didn't want to writhe about on the sofa with this man—with any man.

John was drowning when she moved away from him. He followed her up, his hands still moving intimately on her body, until they were both on their feet. He knew she was about to lead him into her bedroom . . . his eyes were caressing as he half-opened them. He stroked her arms softly and looked into her eyes.

Lucy turned away from the desire in his eyes, suddenly overwhelmed by the terror of her memories.

He wanted to pull her back, love her until her

eyes were drowsy with sex. He wasn't sure what had happened, but he knew that the moment was gone.

'Tomorrow?' he asked.

'Not tomorrow—I'm babysitting for Janice. Call me.'

'I will.'

When he was gone, she locked the door behind him, locking herself into the empty apartment with her memories.

She didn't sleep well. Her dreams were tortured and she tossed, fighting her bedclothes and feeling a hot, stifling trap that was not there. When she got up, she could hear the rain drumming on the roof of the building.

Haunted: her sleep was perpetually haunted by formless dreams. Once she had thought of going to a psychiatrist, trying to escape the haunting, but in the end, she had kept her sleepless nights to herself rather than relive a past she wanted desperately to forget. In Toronto, with Max, the dreams had come less often. She had gradually come to feel that the past was dead, that she was free.

She had been so wrong. As Max came to mean more to her, as she began to feel the desire to respond to him, the nightmares had returned. Finally she had run away rather than deal with her own fears of love, her own memories.

She had coffee and a shower and felt better able to face the day, but nothing could totally disperse the effect of the oppressive rain. The tail end of a spring storm, the weather man had said.

Almost as compensation for the week of rain, he had promised sunshine for the weekend.

'I'll pretend the sun is shining now,' Lucy muttered as she parked her car and dashed through the blowing rain, across the street and into the building where Do-It-Yourself Data Processing was located.

She paused in the foyer, surveying her domain.

She had come to Prince Rupert a year ago, looking for something new, hoping this small city on the wild west coast of Canada would give a challenge to her restless spirit. Being alone and unemployed had frightened her, but she'd been determined to start her own business. She desperately needed to be kept busy, to keep away memories of the past. Her first customer had been happy and he had told his aquaintances. Lucy did a good job for all of them, but she knew she could do more if she expanded with computer equipment. The idea of borrowing money had frightened her, but she had needed a project bigger than her sleepless nights.

She now had four computer booths booked almost to capacity. She could see the light on in one of the booths already. Janice, her bookkeeper, had come in early.

'Morning, Janice!' She locked the door behind herself as it was still too early for clients.

'Hi, Lucy. I thought I'd get in early to finish off the scaling figures that Jack brought in last night. I wanted to get them through before the clients tie up all the machines. I'll leave half an hour early tonight if you don't mind—Shall I stop and make you a coffee?'

'Don't bother, Janice, I'll get it myself.'

While the coffee brewed, Lucy flipped through the computer bookings. A few minutes later, when she placed a cup of the fragrant coffee at Janice's elbow, the small, dark girl looked up with a smile.

'Thanks—Did you have a good time last night?'

'Not bad. Terry Goodwin might come in this week to see about getting us to do his books.'

'I didn't ask about business. What about you and John?'

'It was a nice party.' Lucy picked up the paper as it came off the printer, watching for anything that seemed out of place on the print-out.

'That's not an answer,' grumbled Janice goodnaturedly. 'Are you going out tonight?'

Was everyone in the world hung up on romance? She was making a good life for herself here. Did it have to have love as well? How could it, when she couldn't bear to make love with a man?

'Tonight I'm babysitting for that angel of yours—remember?'

'I don't want to get between you and your love life.' Janice had a husband at home, one she loved. An evening out with her husband would be nice, but she really wanted to see Lucy with a man.

'I've been thinking about modifying the computer program for these scaling calculations,' Lucy told her. 'How long did this run take you?'

Janice let the change of subject go without comment. 'I worked on it for two hours yesterday and half an hour this morning.'

'I think we could do better than that.' Lucy

leaned over the terminal to point out to Janice the changes she had planned. 'Above all, doing it that way would save a lot of time.'

'Where did you learn so much about computer programming?'

'Here and there—I worked in Toronto for a software house for a while.' She didn't want to talk about S.C.S. or about Max. Too many memories—good memories, but ones that were becoming as painful as the bad memories from life with Ted.

What was Max doing now? Had he forgotten her? Had he found another woman—one who could accept his lovemaking with joy instead of fear? Or did he still remember, still want her? If he knew where she was, would he come to her?

Staring at the computer print-outs, she remembered a night in Toronto when she and Max had worked late to find an elusive bug in the payroll program. She had checked print-out after print-out against government tax tables, while Max made changes to the program. The dawn light was in the sky when they finished. Max had left the print-outs on Chan's desk and locked up the office, and they had driven around until they found a restaurant that was open, eating spaghetti at five in the morning, watching the night people.

At the table beside them, three musicians were relaxing after a night of playing for a wedding. They had tossed a friendly comment towards Max and Lucy, high-spirited after their successful night. Max had given a quick reply, inviting the musicians to join them, and Lucy had listened as he drew the band leader out about their wandering life, about their dreams for success. As her interest caught, she started questioning them herself. The five of them had eaten together, talking music and travel, laughing in the early morning.

Later, Max had let her off at her apartment as the neighbours were going to work. The elderly gentleman from the apartment below hers had glanced pointedly at his watch as he passed her coming in. Evidently, he had assumed she had just come home from a night on the town.

'Little does he know,' Max drawled, 'that you've been up all night with a computer. That would really shock him!'

She had looked up at Max's smile, smiling back at him, but resisting the urge to invite him into her apartment. She'd known all along that he desired her, had avoided having him in her apartment for that reason—and because she didn't want to destroy their friendship. If Max had reached for her, wanting her, she had known she would be unable to handle the situation with any sort of sophistication. Damn Max for not letting her forget him! If only she could leave him in the past where he belonged! She concentrated hard on what Janice was saying.

'—to the new medical centre this afternoon, but Dr Fletcher called to say he's had to do emergency surgery and can he cancel until tomorrow. Lucy, you've been working so many nights, why don't you take the afternoon off?'

'I can't. The Princess Fishery people are coming this morning, and by noon I'll have enough on my desk to keep me busy for a week. Beside, it's raining outside—not the best weather for a day off.' Work was better therapy for her than idleness.

'That rain is sure getting me down,' grumbled Janice as she turned back to her desk.

Lucy went into her office, mentally organising her day. At nine Cheryl, the receptionist, came in. Then the clients started coming.

Janice called for help at nine-thirty. A client had ignored the instructions in the manual and done the month-end process for his company's books in the wrong order. It wasn't a mistake he was likely to make again—not after spending the morning retyping most of yesterday's work to recover the error.

At ten the men from Princess Fishery came in. The little man did all the talking, his darting eyes never meeting Lucy's. His companion sat silently uncomfortable in a chair that seemed too small.

Lucy suppressed her excitement as she listened to them, keeping her voice calm as she discussed the possibility that they might purchase several microcomputers which could handle their processing, also acting as terminals for the computer in Vancouver when required.

'I'm only speculating about what might suit you,' she concluded. 'If I'm to recommend a system for you, I'll have to come down and take a look at your operation.' They liked that idea—at least, the little spokesman liked it. Lucy agreed to accept the job of drawing up a proposal for them for what she privately thought was an outrageous fee. As she watched the two men leave the room, she had a sudden urge to call Max, to tell him about this development. Instead, she called Cheryl for a cup of coffee.

Would Max ever get out of her head? She had run away from him a year ago, but he was still there as strongly as ever. Recently, she had fancied he was in her mind more than ever—as if he were only in the next room. It was possible that Max would be there for the rest of her life, a symbol of what she could never have.

At twelve Janice looked in to ask her if she was coming to lunch. She realised that she was starving, but didn't want to stop working.

'I'll stay,' she decided. 'Could you pick me up a sandwich?'

'Ham? Or egg salad?' The lunch room Janice frequented had a limited menu.

'Ham, please.'

When Janice returned, she quietly placed the sandwich on Lucy's desk. Lucy ate it without realising it was smoked beef, not ham. When five o'clock came, she felt she had earned a night off. Through the day, despite interruptions, she had managed to clear most of the work off her desk and make a good start on the Princess Fishery work. She had also developed a pounding headache.

She took two aspirins before leaving the office. Across the street, she ate alone at a table for two. The waitress commented on the weather, and Lucy agreed that they certainly hadn't had much sunshine this spring.

After the solitary dinner, she went to Janice's house with some eagerness. She always enjoyed young Amanda.

'Jim's still in the shower,' Janice greeted her at the door. 'Come in and have a drink with me while we wait.'

In the living room, Janice sat back in an easy chair, watching her boss play with her baby daughter.

Lucy ducked her face behind her hands, and Amanda gurgled in anticipation.

'Peek-a-boo!' announced Lucy, pulling her hands away, while Amanda bounced up and down with delight.

'You should get married and have your own,' Janice told her. 'You should marry John.'

'I'm not going to marry John.' Lucy lifted the baby's hands in front of her chubby young face. She shivered, remembering the feel of John's hands on her.

'Boo!' announced Amanda.

'Who, then? You're twenty-seven years old, Lucy. You can't wait for ever—what about Max?'

Lucy's arms froze in the act of picking up the baby.

'Max?'

'You mention him sometimes.'

Did she? Had Max been appearing in her conversations without her knowledge? She knew Max kept popping back into her thoughts, but she hadn't realised that she talked about him. She felt the baby squirm in her arms and she looked at Amanda. If she had been able to stay in Toronto—if she had been able to accept Max's desire for her—would they have married and had a child? Would a child made by her and Max have looked anything like this baby in her arms? Crazy thoughts, dreaming about the impossible.

'There's no one, Janice. I don't want there to be anyone.' She knew as she said it that it was not true. She could hardly deny wanting Max, despite the impossibility of it all.

'Who's here? Jim stood in the doorway, freshly shaven, his red hair still wet from the shower.

'Are you ready to go yet, Janice? Let's go—Hi, Lucy!'

'Am *I* ready?' spluttered Janice. 'You're the big lug who spent the last half hour in the shower!'

Man and wife smiled at each other, belying the tone of their bickering.

When they had gone, Lucy ran a bath for Amanda. She played with the baby in the bathroom until they were both soaking wet, then dried Mandy and dressed her in a clean nappy and pyjamas before putting her to bed.

She looked at the young charmer in her crib. Janice was wrong. Certainly Lucy enjoyed Amanda, had the maternal urges that made caring for the baby a satisfying experience; but that didn't mean she needed motherhood—or a husband. She had a full and satisfying life. How many married women were free as Lucy was—free to enjoy a career, yet free to move on when they became restless.

After cleaning Amanda's splashes from the bathroom walls and floor, Lucy browsed through Janice's bookshelves until she found a good book. She settled on the sofa to read, carefully keeping her thoughts on the book.

When Janice and Jim returned, she greeted them sleepily.

'Your daughter was an angel,' she announced. 'I'm going home to bed.'

For the first time in months she slept soundly and dreamlessly, arriving at work the next day with no suspicion of what was in store for her.

It began as a normal day, busy and varied. Lucy did some work on the computer until things got busy, then she retreated to her office to work on ideas for the Princess Fishery proposal.

Some time after ten the telephone at her elbow rang. She answered it, her eyes still on the papers.

'About dinner at my place tonight?' John began. 'You said to call you—how about it? Are you free tonight?'

Was she free? Was John a helpful diversion, or was he about to become a problem, with his advances? He had all the symptoms of getting serious about her, and she should stop that before it was too late. Then she thought of spending the evening alone with her ghosts and shuddered. 'All right, John. I'll come in my own car but I'll have to leave early to come back here and do some work. Seven o'clock?'

'Why not earlier? You can put your feet up and relax.'

She laughed. 'We'll compromise. I'll come between six-thirty and seven, but I'll have to leave early.' Cheryl appeared in the doorway, hovering, waiting for Lucy to be finished on the telephone. 'I'll say goodbye now, John—I have a client waiting.'

'There's a man here,' Cheryl announced as Lucy replaced the receiver. 'He wants to know what brand of computer you use and I told him. He wants to know if he can use a modem. What's a modem?'

'It's for allowing computers to talk to each other on the phone lines,' said Lucy. 'Janice can talk to him. She knows how to use the modem.'

'He says he wants to talk to you about it.'

She should have known then who the man was, but no warning bell rang.

'Tell him I'll be out in a minute.'

She closed the door to her office as she came out, thinking that she would go to lunch once she had dealt with the modem man. He wasn't in the foyer. She raised her brows at Cheryl, and the receptionist gestured towards the nearest computer booth.

The floors were covered with soft static proof carpet, and her shoes moved silently into the booth.

She knew him as soon as she saw him. He was turned away from her, his hands in his pockets, his dark head bent as he studied the scene outside the window. Lucy had to work to suppress a gasp. She felt as if she had been punched in the stomach. She barely had time to hide the look of shock on her face before he turned.

In the past, Max had often been smiling at her, but today there was no smile on his face. 'I wondered if it was you. I saw the name on the door—L. Carter, Certified General Accountant. It had to be you.'

He hadn't changed. His face might be slightly thinner, but he had been lean when she knew him. Standing less than four feet from him, she felt an awareness of every inch of him. Nothing had changed about Max McGraw.

Lucy had her face under control. When her voice came it was husky, but it didn't tremble.

'Hello, Max.'

For the life of her, she couldn't think of another word to say to him. He watched her silently for a moment, his eyes dark.

'Why did you run away, Lucy?'

'Run?' She tried to make it sound like an

innocent query. 'It's my pattern, Max. You knew it when you hired me. I don't stay long; I get restless.' How could she explain her reasons? Why had she run? Because he came too close to her, made her feel too much. But to tell him that would be dangerous, would reveal too much to him.

'Yes,' he agreed, 'but you left the other jobs smoothly, finishing the job properly and helping your replacement fit in. Lucy, I didn't expect that you would just disappear. When I left you in your apartment that night, I knew we had problems to work out, but you didn't stay to work them out. You ran.'

She felt a momentary resentment that he had been checking up on her past, then realised he had probably checked her references when she applied for a job with his firm. What he said was true. She'd been restless, but she'd been careful to maintain her professional standing and not to leave hard feelings behind her.

'Max——' she shook her head, 'I'm sorry, but——'

'Why did you run away?'

She had no answer to give him. She tried to change the subject.

'Cheryl said you wanted to use a modem. You can use the system by the window. There's a modem there—the same type you have at S.C.S., so you'll have no problem operating it.' She told him the hourly charge for the use of the system and turned away, hoping to get out of the door before he stopped her.

'Lucy!'

Against her will, her body turned back towards

him. He was still standing where she had first seen him. Except to turn towards her, he had not moved.

'We're going to resolve this situation between us, Lucy. You're not going to run away this time.'

She didn't run; she walked away. Cheryl was at the switchboard. With the soundproofed baffles placed around each computer system, there was some chance that the receptionist hadn't overheard her conversation with Max.

'Mr McGraw will be using system number three. When's the next booking for it?' Although she knew her hands were trembling, her voice was steady.

Cheryl consulted the booking sheet on her desk. 'Two o'clock this afternoon. Metlakatla Construction will be doing their accounts receivable.'

'Tell Janice about Mr McGraw,' instructed Lucy. 'If he's still on number three at one-thirty, she should let him know that the system is booked for two o'clock. I'll be out for the afternoon. Tell Janice.'

Running again, taunted a small voice inside her. It was Max's voice.

CHAPTER TWO

THE government docks were below the city, past the canneries on the waterfront road. Fleeing from Max's unexpected reappearance in her life, Lucy went instinctively to the water. Through all the years of her childhood she had lived on boats. When she was troubled or worried, she had walked the docks, looking at the other boats, thinking, dreaming.

Climbing down the ramp, she ridiculed herself for tramping the wharves in high-heeled shoes and a tight skirt. If she wasn't careful, she would slip and fall on the wet planks. Serve her right if she broke a leg.

The rain no longer fell, and the wind had calmed. To the west she could see the promise of a clear sky, but overhead the grey clouds still threatened another spring storm.

She walked slowly, looking the boats over. She had done this so often with her parents when she was young. In the evening, after a day's sailing, they had tied up to some strange dock and stretched their legs. She eyed the big fishing boat at the end of the first finger of the wharf, wondering how it would have seemed to her father.

'Seaworthy,' he would have approved. He would have paced it off on the dock to see if it really was the sixty feet he estimated. He would have approved the high bulwarks around the decks, but would have shaken his head at the large wheelhouse windows. 'All right on the coast, but not for the open sea. One good ocean wave would take that window away.'

Her mother would have agreed, smiling indulgently while keeping an eye out for other live-aboard women to gossip with.

Once Lucy and Max had gone to a marina on Lake Ontario. They had been working on computer programs for the owners, but as they worked she had been aware of the boats outside the office window.

'Let's go sightseeing!' Max had suggested when they finished their work.

It was a magic afternoon. They had walked the docks slowly, looking at little boats and big boats. Max had pointed out one big sailing schooner.

'See her port of registry—she's from London. I'll bet they've crossed the Atlantic not long ago. Let's see!' He had knocked on the hull of the boat to rouse the occupants.

He was right. The young couple had sailed across the Atlantic with their three children, then journeyed up the St Lawrence Seaway to the Great Lakes. They invited Max and Lucy aboard. Max helped Lucy step up on to the deck, but she didn't object, didn't tell him that she had done this many times before.

Inside the yacht, he had retained his grip on her hand. She had started to tug it away, but he had shaken his head, smiling at her, and it seemed silly to make a fuss. She had subsided, sitting with him on the salon settee. When they had listened to the tale of the schooner's travels,

Max turned to Lucy.

'What do you think, Lucy? Shall we buy ourselves a sailing vessel and cast off? Bermuda . . . the Bahamas . . . through the Panama Canal and on to the South Pacific.'

'Or north to the west coast of Canada,' she had continued his fantasy. Of course it was a fantasy. Max was tied to Toronto and S.C.S. 'I've never been to the west coast, never visited British Columbia or Alaska.'

'Out there,' the skipper of this schooner told them, 'you want a warm stove on board.'

'The wood stove you have in your salon must be ideal.' Max admired the miniature cast-iron stove, while Lucy sat back and let the skipper's wife serve her coffee, listening to the men talk, listening to the noise of the children in the forward cabin.

Later, on their way back to the office, Max had offered, 'Come sailing with me, Lucy. I've got a little day sailer. My son and I go out on it most weekends. Come with us this weekend—I'll teach you how to hoist a sail.'

She would have loved to go sailing with him, but she didn't go. She didn't tell him she already knew how to hoist sails. She imagined she knew what his day sailer would be like. Big enough for now, he'd told her; something to practise with and have fun until he got the big boat he dreamed of.

She evaded Max that time, but later she couldn't evade him any more—except by running.

She walked away from the big fishing boat, putting Max back in his place—wherever that was. Somewhere in the back of her mind? Always waiting for an unwary moment?

Three fishermen were working at net mending. A black net was spread out all along the length of the fifth finger. Lucy edged her way along it as far as she could. She smiled at the young fisherman with the tousled black hair.

'Yours?' he asked, jerking his head towards a big sailboat at the far end of the finger.

'No—just looking. Mind if I walk across your net?'

'Bad luck for a woman to walk on the net.' He smiled at her then. 'Go ahead.' He gestured where she should walk and she went carefully, wishing again for flat-heeled sneakers instead of high-heeled shoes.

The big boat was a live-aboard. You wouldn't hesitate to cross an ocean in her. She wondered about the people who were lucky enough to own her. Lucy guessed it was a forty-five-footer. She would have paced it off to be sure, but couldn't pace through the jumble of black net on the dock.

Her name was *Wanderlust*. Her hull was dark blue. She had teak decks and two beautifully varnished wooden masts. She was ketch-rigged. Lucy knew the narrow bow would slice the water cleanly; she'd sail like a dream.

'Like her?'

The sailor on the deck of the ketch had unruly brown hair curling over the neck of his bulky fisherman's sweater. He wasn't more than twelve years old.

'I like her. How does she sail?'

'Easy. She cruises about eight knots with full sail and a steady wind. She's not too stiff.' A stiff, quick motion could make a boat miserable to sail for her owners. This young sailor knew that already.

'Where'd you come from?' asked Lucy.

The trailboards proclaimed her as the *Wanderlust*, her home port as Vancouver. With a boat like this, Lucy knew she could as easily have arrived from Tahiti as from five hundred miles south on the Canadian coast.

'My dad bought her in Vancouver and we sailed the open Pacific up to Alaska. We've just come from Alaska now. It's two months since we left Vancouver. We got here yesterday, and was it ever wild! We crossed Chatham Sound with the main down, under mizzen and staysail. We were roaring along like you wouldn't believe.'

'I'd believe it. They say the west coast of Canada is wilder than anywhere else in the world. Where do you go next?'

'Dad doesn't know yet. Do you want to see inside?'

Lucy shook her head. This young sailor was friendly, but his parents could be another story . . . and, somehow, she didn't want to put faces to the owners of *Wanderlust*. She was too much like the boat of Lucy's dreams . . .

The Frasers' house was on Fourth Avenue, an area of Prince Rupert that Lucy loved. The street wound high over the city, giving the residents in their big old houses a spectacular view of the ocean harbour. Tonight, however, the rainclouds hung low over the city. The harbour below was obscured, leaving the Fraser house as a haven against the chilly, wet weather. A place to hide in.

Marg, John's mother, settled Lucy in the living

room with a hot cup of coffee and a soft, comfortable, overstuffed chair. She refused Lucy's offer to help with dinner.

'It's all done, Lucy. We're having a lazy meal—Shake-and-Bake chicken and baked potatoes. It's all in the oven and the table is set. I'm even free to have a cup of coffee with you while we wait. Just sit and relax. John says you've been working much too hard lately.'

'I enjoy being busy. Where's John?'

'He just slipped down to the store for me, he'll be back any minute. John says you have to go back to work tonight. Couldn't you take the evening off and relax?'

'You tempt me.' Lucy leaned back into the comfortable chair and let her body relax. 'This room gives such a feeling of coming home after a hard day that I'll hate to leave it. I'm glad you lit the fire.'

The fireplace flames licked softly at the air, sending warm red glints to the metal surfaces of the copper tea service on a nearby table. The warm varnish of the antique end tables caught the light of the fire.

John's mother completed the image. Her soft, greying hair topped a serene face. The embodiment of the perfect mother. Lucy felt strange in this environment, as if she were only pretending to fit in . . . only pretending that Max hadn't walked back into her life today. Where was Max at this moment?

'Where is your home, Lucy?' The question came almost as if John's mother sensed Lucy's feelings.

'I have no family left.' She had a sudden, vivid

vision of the Caribbean . . . blue skies . . . blue seas . . . sudden, wild destructive storms. After the Caribbean had come the loneliness, then Ted.

Outside, a car door slammed.

'Don't be concerned, Lucy,' said Marg. 'There's no need for you to talk about painful subjects.'

There were entirely too many astute people in the world, thought Lucy as she sipped her coffee. Or was she not as good as she thought at hiding her distress at questions about the past? She must hide her feelings better, she thought, smiling warmly for John as he came into the room.

He seemed to fit with the room, his smooth good looks doing nothing to upset the feeling of calm.

'How was your day?' he asked Lucy.

'Not bad.' She thought of mentioning Princess Fishery, but decided against it. Prince Rupert was a very small city. 'I had a busy morning, but I took this afternoon off. While the rest of the town worked, I strolled around the docks and looked at boats.'

Marg sat up with interest. 'John's father and I used to love wandering around the floats on a nice evening. There weren't as many visitors then, but I loved to see them all.'

John chuckled, 'I remember. You always felt the people on the boats that had just arrived must be hungry and dirty, and you were forever inviting them home for a bath and dinner.'

'A good idea,' commented Lucy. 'You can eat well off the ocean, but many boats are too small to have a shower. There were some nice boats today. There was a beautiful ketch—a two-masted sailboat. With her wooden masts and bronze portholes, she looked almost like a pirate boat.'

'Where was it from?' asked Marg.

'She's registered as *Wanderlust* from Vancouver, but she's just come from Alaska. Can you imagine what it would be like to be cruising? I was talking to a fisherman who'd just brought in a catch of salmon from the Queen Charlotte Islands. This bad weather is only local. Once you get outside Rupert Harbour the sun is shining.'

John nodded. 'The mountains around the harbour tend to hold the clouds when they come in from the Pacific Ocean. Five miles west of here you can probably see every star in the sky.'

Lucy's eyes were filled with dreams, and Marg teased, 'You could hire on as crew on that sailboat, Lucy—spend the rest of the summer cruising.'

As she had spent so many summers in her childhood. Those days of sun and laughter and the love of her parents seemed far away beyond reach. Yet wouldn't it be wonderful if she could recapture that feeling?

'And what about her business?' asked John.

'Let me dream of a sail on the Pacific . . . moonlit nights . . . waves lapping against the hull as the boat racks softly.'

Lucy was smiling as if at a secret; John experienced again that fleeting that she might slip away from him. Marg, the perfect hostess, decided it was time to serve dinner.

Later, John tried to keep Lucy, but she insisted that she couldn't duck work—not after taking the afternoon off.

'I wish I didn't have to,' she told him as he opened the front door to let her leave. It wasn't true. She wanted to go to the office, to bury herself in work. She shivered in her light raincoat. 'It's raining again. What a spring! Will it ever stop?'

'Perhaps not for a while,' he told her. He would have liked to be able to tell her that the sun would shine tomorrow, but a look at the sky would have made a liar of him.

'Well, I've no choice. I'd better get it done.'

She smiled at him and was gone before he could kiss her good night. A dirty trick, she supposed. She'd taken John's hospitality and enjoyed his home and his mother. And John. She could sense in him a desire to deepen their relationship. John was certainly a man she should be able to trust, but——

Janice had a good relationship, seemed to be happy with a man she loved. But for Lucy, that kind of love wasn't possible any more. After her disastrous marriage with Ted, how could she bring herself to trust another person with her welfare? She knew she could never regain that innocent trust, yet somehow she kept wishing, hoping. Seeing couples like Janice and Jim, happy in their loving partnership, stirred her restlessness. If she could only learn to be content with what she had, perhaps even the dreams would stop. She had to be content; had to convince Max that she didn't need him.

She drove quickly to the office, knowing she was speeding and risking being stopped by the police, but hardly caring. Inside, she locked the door behind herself and turned on only one light.

She switched on the power bar for the computer and loaded the scaling program from the disk into the computer's memory, then stared at the opening lines of the program listing.

When she was a teenager, sailing in the West Indies, the waves had lapped gently against the boat. The water had been warmed by the blazing sun overhead. They had cruised in and out of the islands, exploring and absorbing the life of the people who lived there. Then, one week, Lucy had accepted an invitation to stay with friends.

While she was on shore, the unexpected tropical storm had blown up out of nowhere, demolishing the harbour and the boats lying at anchor there. Afterwards, searchers found pieces of debris from the yacht that had been Lucy's home, but no sign of her mother or father. The fifteen-year-old Lucy was taken in charge by the American Consulate and sent to her mother's sister in California. Aunt Winifred received Lucy with icy coolness and promptly sent her off to boarding school. The year she graduated, Lucy finally escaped her lonely existence by marrying Ted Carter, the brother of a school friend.

The marriage was a disaster. Two years after marrying Ted, Lucy left California, desperately trying to escape from her husband. She had been barely eighteen when she married; she was twenty when she left Ted. In the time between, she had learned that the world was not a gentle place, that men were not always protectors—that they were to be feared.

She went north to Canada. She didn't know if Ted would look for her, but she knew he must not find her. She chose Canada because it was north, and all the places she had talked about to Ted were to the south.

She had been brought up knowing that she would marry one day, as her mother had done, but nothing had prepared her for a situation where she would be alone and unable to call on anyone for help.

She crossed the border at Vancouver and found a job there answering telephones in an accountant's office. The immigration authorities agreed to let her stay as a landed immigrant. Once across the border, she felt safer.

In Canada, and all around the world, the employment situation was worsening. Lucy had obtained her job partly because of her pleasant speaking voice and good looks, but, if the firm she was working for had to lay off employees, she felt she would be the first to go.

She set to work to increase her value to her employer. She took typing at night school, then registered as a correspondence student in the Certified General Accountants programme. She managed the fees by cutting down on her grocery bill; by walking to work instead of taking the bus.

She left Vancouver two years later with a glowing reference from her employers. The job she found in Saskatchewan was higher paid. She continued her studies and worked hard, then moved again with another good reference.

She knew the restlessness was a hindrance to her career, but she found it unbearable to stay in one place too long. Each new job, each new place, was stimulating to her. While she was working hard, learning new things, she had no time to feel lonely. She dreamed, of course, but at least the days passed quickly. When time passed and the newness wore off, she became aware of the emptiness again. Then the wanderlust would take hold of her and she would move on.

She was working for an accounting firm in a small town north of Lake Superior when she saw Max's advertisement in a Toronto newspaper. She had the accounting knowledge he was asking for, but her computer knowledge was hazy at best. One of her accounting courses had dealt with computers, and she had once attended a two-day seminar for her employer in Saskatchewan. She had learned a little theory, but had only once touched a computer.

She had a week off coming to her and she used it, typing a résumé and taking the train to Toronto to present it in person. She knew her qualifications on paper were unlikely to get her the job; she had to try to sell herself in person.

When she arrived in Toronto, she registered in a hotel. She freshened up before going to apply for the job. The office was in downtown Toronto. The building was modern and sterile, with fast elevators and large windows tinted against the sun's rays. When Lucy found the right floor, she pushed open a door and found a totally different atmosphere inside.

The receptionist's office was carpeted, with several doors opening from it, and there were some plants to lend atmosphere. Lucy's attention was instantly caught by the wall behind the receptionist, where an oil painting depicted a sailing boat racing along on a blue sea with a few fast-moving clouds overhead. She imagined she could hear the water, feel the motion of that vessel underfoot.

The chairs in the receptionist's area were comfortable enough to be very expensive. In a room beyond, she could see two men on a comfortable settee, intently studying a sheaf of papers on the table in front of them. Beyond the men, she saw a computer terminal.

She sensed an atmosphere of relaxed determination. She was to learn that it was a frame of mind typical of Max McGraw; to calmly work on towards his goal, hardly bothered by the obstacles in front of him.

Lucy's hopes of getting in to see Max that day were dashed.

'He won't be seeing anyone today. Leave your résumé, and leave a number where you can be reached while you're in town. If possible, he'll call you tomorrow.' The girl was friendly but firm. Lucy speculated that Mr McGraw probably had one of the best secretaries in Toronto.

She waited in her room the next day, not wanting to risk being out if anyone called her about the job. It was late in the afternoon before she finally received a call from the secretary. Mr McGraw would see Ms Carter the next day at ten in the morning.

When she entered the office the next morning, she had had time to become nervous and apprehensive about the interview.

She recognised Max McGraw as one of the two men she had seen the day before. He interviewed her in the same room, seating her on the sofa and himself across from her in an easy chair. His desk was by the window, filled with a computer terminal and papers from some project.

The secretary brought coffee for them both,

then closed the door, leaving them alone. Lucy was to learn later that Max rarely closed the door that separated him from his staff; that the sofa she sat on was frequently the location for brainstorming, for lengthy discussions when there were problems with a program.

She judged that he was in his mid-thirties. He was attractive, well dressed in the casual clothes that were beginning to become acceptable in much of the business world. She put him down as a married man because he didn't have a predatory gleam in his eye. Later, she found she was partly wrong. He was widowed and had a ten-year-old son.

He introduced himself and told her a bit about the company. When he started asking questions, she had become quite relaxed with him, no longer on her guard. He questioned her easily, almost carelessly, but within five minutes she felt that he had pumped her of everything she knew. Despite his friendly, relaxed manner, he hadn't missed a word she had said, hadn't forgotten to ask about any aspect of her past experience. Those dark eyes of his had missed nothing.

She sensed that he was going to send her away and file her application in the waste basket, so she spoke quickly, hoping to influence his decision.

'I don't have a background in computers, but I feel I have a good grasp of the basic concepts from the course I took, and I think I could learn quickly if I were given the chance. You're working mainly on payroll programs here. I have experience with a wide variety of payroll types, and I think I could do the job. I'd certainly like to try.'

'Ms Carter,' he mocked gently, 'I'm not much of a believer in theory courses in computers. The best way to learn about computers is hands-on, by using them. I once hired a fellow on the strength of his excellent marks in a college computer course, only to find he was terrified to touch a keyboard.' Lucy sensed that he was not unsympathetic, but that he did not intend to hire her.

'Mr McGraw, if you did hire me—if this were my first day, what would you be wanting me to do?'

'I'd put you at a computer and give you our payroll program. I'd ask you to try it out, study the manual and learn how to use the program.' He set down his cup, a look of finality on his face. 'I don't doubt your abilities, but I need someone to help reduce my own work load. I don't have time to give basic lessons in how to use a computer.'

'Why not give me the program and the manual right now—let me try?'

She had sparked his interest. He hesitated, then moved to a bookcase where he selected a leather-bound manual. From his desk he took a sheaf of papers.

'Why not?' he grinned. 'If nothing else, you can put a brief experience with payroll data processing on your résumé. The program disks are inside the binder. There's a computer in the next office that you can use. If you get it figured out, you might try running this payroll through and printing out pay statements.'

Lucy took the things he was handing her and followed him out of the room into an adjoining office, where he showed her the computer. 'Do you want me to close the door?'

'Yes, please.' This computer was not the same as the one she had briefly used in her course. She had no idea how to turn it on and she certainly didn't want witnesses. Max McGraw didn't offer to help, but left her alone in the room.

Luckily, the manual had an excellent index. She got the computer turned on and the program started. Then, step by step, she went through the manual, pushing the appropriate buttons on the computer as she was told to.

When noon came she was hungry, but she was afraid to leave to eat in case she was unable to get back to work afterwards. By one o'clock she was entering the data for the payroll Max McGraw had given her, marvelling at the speed with which the computer calculated each employee's pay cheque.

There was a box of continuous feed cheques under the printer table, but she didn't know if she could succeed in loading the printer properly, so she printed the cheques on the plain white paper that was already in the printer. She went on to the month-end procedure, then the year-end. She was wondering if she should try to change the paper for the government T4 forms when Max came in.

He looked through her print-outs without comment, then set down the papers and looked at her. He was smiling slightly, and she realised then just how badly she wanted to get this job.

'I must admit I'm surprised,' he said. 'What do you think of the program?'

'I found it straightforward—the directions that appear on the computer screen are very helpful.

Of course, anyone who had done payroll manually would be impressed by how quickly the computer does it.' He was waiting for more, so she went on. 'I thought the overtime section could be expanded. There doesn't seem to be any allowance for piece rates. Perhaps that could be built into the overtime section.'

'How?' He wasn't giving anything away, and Lucy wondered if she had just ruined whatever small chance she had for the job.

She picked up a paper and pencil and roughed out the idea that had occurred to her while she was using the program. She knew little about computer programming, but she did know accounting and she thought what she was proposing couldn't be too difficult.

Max eyed the rough sketch she had made, and she held her breath until he looked up at her.

'Any other ideas?' he asked.

'Just a small one. I think you should lengthen the field for the company's name. Lots of businesses have longer names than that.'

He nodded. 'Actually, we've already done that. A few customers had complained about there not being enough room to put in their names.' He eyed her cautiously. 'I admit I'm impressed, but I'm hesitant about your lack of experience. Would you consider the job on a one-month trial basis?'

'Yes,' she replied instantly.

'Are you sure? You've got a job right now. If you leave it to come here, you could end up out on the street in a month's time.'

She took a deep breath, realising she had won. She smiled at him. 'There's no danger of that. I'm going to make myself indispensable to you!'

CHAPTER THREE

MAX made S.C.S. a good place to work. He took pride in turning out a quality product, and made sure that everyone who worked with him felt the same. The people around him sometimes became excited, arguing about the best way to program a module, whether sufficient testing had been done. Max listened to it all, used the good ideas, devastated the bad ideas with a few quiet words, and managed to inspire total loyalty in them all.

At the end of Lucy's first month Max handed her a pay cheque. There was no talk of her leaving. As the following months went by, she began to feel that she might stay, make a home. She bought a small car and began to have thoughts about buying a small house. It was the first time since leaving Ted that she had been able to believe she might settle down happily.

She worked hard, often staying late when she became involved in a project. She and Max spent a good deal of time together, testing and making modifications to the programs, and she quickly came to feel that he was her friend as well as her employer. If she ever needed help, Max McGraw would be a good person to turn to.

Chan, Max's assistant programmer, had spent one week looking like death, worried about something he could not share with anyone. One morning he walked into Max's office, closing the door behind himself. Neither Max nor Chan ever mentioned what had happened behind that closed door, but when Chan came out, the sick look was gone. Following that incident, Chan became Max's staunchest defender, bristling whenever Wendy, the secretary, showed the slightest resentment at having to stay late when she had a date.

When they had a deadline, everyone worked late. Other times, Lucy and Max became involved in projects and simply forgot the time. The first time it happened, he invited her to dinner when they finally stopped working.

'There's no need,' she told him. 'I'll get something at home.'

He grimaced, 'But I won't. David, my son, is at my mother's apartment, and they've already had dinner by now. If I turn up hungry, my mother will cook a three-course meal and make me feel guilty as hell! On the other hand, if I go to a restaurant by myself, I'll be staring at the walls thinking about computers. Besides, I owe you at least a dinner for all the extra hours you've been putting in.'

'I've a feeling you're frightened of your mother.'

'Terrified,' he agreed.

She went with him. She thought he would go to a quiet, classy place where she would feel out of place, but he took her instead to an Italian restaurant where the pasta was delicious and the owner greeted Max enthusiastically. He eyed Lucy appreciatively and winked at Max.

'This one you should hang on to, Max! She's got something special!'

Max smiled and held the chair for Lucy. 'Maybe I should, Joe.'

Lucy was stiff and cold when Max sat opposite her. She stared down at the menu that had appeared in front of her, uncomfortably aware of Max watching her.

'Max, when you asked me to dinner, I didn't think—I mean, I——'

He held up a hand to stop her. 'Joe has been giving me a hard time for ages. David and I come here for supper most Sundays. Joe thinks a boy should have a mother, so he's appointed himself head matchmaker.'

'Oh.' She cursed herself for jumping to conclusions. She was so defensive when it came to man-woman relationships.

'But,' he continued, 'I agree with him that I shouldn't let you go. Ever since you started working at S.C.S., I've been thankful you didn't let me send you away. These last few months we've accomplished more than I ever dreamed possible. We work well together.' He reached across the table and touched her hand. 'I believe in hanging on to my friends, too. We are friends, aren't we, Lucy?'

His hand was gone almost before she could move away from it. He was right: she had come to value his friendship, would hate to lose it. But she was wary, too.

'Yes,' she agreed slowly, 'we're friends.'

'Good!' He lifted his menu. 'Now I'll tell you what you should order. Joe's kitchen produces the best pasta in Toronto!'

As usual, he was right: the food was wonderful. While they ate, Max told Lucy about places she should see in Toronto and she told him where she had already been. They talked about books and movies. They agreed that Agatha Christie was their favourite mystery author—they had both felt a sense of loss at her death—and Lucy confessed to a secret fondness for *Star Wars* movies.

'I have the advantage over you,' Max informed her. 'I can pretend to be going to *Star Wars* because of David. Nobody need know that I enjoy Luke Skywalker as much as he does!'

She couldn't remember when she had laughed so much. It was dark outside when he took her back to the office building where her car was parked. Max pulled up beside her car.

'Will you join David and me for dinner on Sunday, Lucy?' He pulled on the parking brake and shifted his stick shift into neutral. 'We'd enjoy having you.'

Lucy fumbled with the buttons on her coat. 'No, Max, I'm busy on Sunday. Thank you for dinner—it was great pasta!' She smiled at him and slipped out of the bucket seat.

It was true that she was busy. Sundays she spent working on her assignments for her correspondence courses. But that Sunday, she was more aware than usual of the emptiness of her apartment. She wondered if she should get a cat; whether the people who managed the apartment building would object to a cat.

The dinners become a habit. She evaded all other invitations from Max, but he seemed unaffected by her refusals and continued to invite her to movies, to evenings with David and his mother, to go on sailing trips. She said no to them all. Over the months, the friendship between them grew, but Lucy became aware of a look in his eyes that was more than friendliness. If she gave him any encouragement at all, she felt he would take advantage of it.

She was aware of the inconsistency of her actions. She could never let herself fall in love with a man again. Love was an emotion that she had banned from her life. At the same time, she valued those dinners with Max, couldn't make herself give them up. She knew that he was coming to want much more than friendship, but she felt safe so long as she did not accept any other invitations from him. Illogically, the fact that she drove herself home in her own car was symbolic to her.

Perhaps it was symbolic to Max as well.

When her car was in the garage for a tune-up, it seemed silly to refuse Max's invitation for another late evening dinner. They had been experimenting with restaurants, visiting Joe's place frequently, at other times sampling eating places all over Toronto. That night they picked what might have been the worst restaurant in Toronto. The waitress jumbled their order hopelessly and somehow it became a comedy of errors, so that they were suppressing laughter whenever the inept girl returned to their table.

They were still laughing when Max parked outside Lucy's apartment building. It was cool outside the car and the heater was blowing warm air on to her legs. She didn't want to open the car door yet.

'I thought I'd die laughing when she poured your coffee into your dinner,' she giggled. 'There can't be a worse waitress in all Toronto!'

'Or a worse cook. My veal cutlets tasted like leather shoelaces.'

They were silent for a moment, warm and companionable, then Max moved towards her.

'Max,' she whispered. Where was her voice? She wanted to stop him, wanted to push him away, but her hands wouldn't obey her brain's order. Her throat was frozen.

When his lips touched hers, it was like a shock through her body, and she trembled as he touched her. His kiss was warm and gentle, sending waves of feeling through her body. Feelings she didn't want, couldn't handle.

When he drew back, her eyes were wide and alarmed. She shook her head slowly at him.

'No, Max, we can't . . . no——'

He brushed her cheek with his hand, his eyes intent on her in the moonlight. 'Is there someone else? You're not seeing any other man?'

'No,' she denied, 'there is no one.'

'Someone in the past?'

She didn't reply, but he knew.

'You can't hang on to the past, Lucy. It's time to let it go.' He bent to her again and she couldn't move away when his lips explored hers. 'It's time our relationship progressed to the next stage,' he told her.

'No, Max, it can't.' She placed her hand on his arm, pleading with him, 'Don't spoil our friendship, please. I can't be anybody's lover,' she told him as she slipped out of the seat. 'Good night, Max.'

When she was in her apartment, she sat on the sofa in the dark. Alone.

She was alarmed by her body's reaction to

Max's kiss. Following that night, she kept her conversations with him strictly to business and avoided working late. Max must have noticed her coolness, but he said nothing. When Lucy realised that he seemed to have abandoned pursuit, she slowly relaxed. When, finally, they worked late together one night, she forgot to protest at being taken to dinner afterwards.

She enjoyed it. But she drove home in her own car after they had eaten.

Since the time when Max had first kissed her, Lucy's nights had become increasingly disturbed. She resumed her dinners with him, but there was a tension in her that did not dissipate. In her dreams Max often bent towards her as he had that night in his car, but when she moved away from him it was Ted's face that she saw. She would wake terrified, remembering those years with Ted.

When she had completed the last course in her five-year Certified General Accountants' programme, Max insisted that she have the day off.

'You've earned it. Take the day, go sightseeing, do some shopping. Then go home and soak in a hot tub. I'll pick you up at seven and take you out for a celebration. Don't shake your head at me, Lucy. This time you're saying yes! Now, go off and enjoy your day. I'll see you at seven.'

He had turned away, leaving her alone in her office. She could have—should have—gone after him and protested, but instead, she got her handbag and her coat and left the building. Just one evening. She would go out with him just once on a real date. One time wouldn't hurt.

It was a magic evening. Lucy was glad she had

bought a new dress that afternoon. Max took her to an elegant night club on top of a downtown hotel, where they ate and danced. She relaxed in his arms as they moved to the music, convincing herself that it really was magic, that it wasn't real.

Later, at her door, she should have said good night, but instead, she had invited him in. Inside, she had surrendered to a heady dream world where the feel of his arms and his lips had caught at some wild part of her and left her wanting nothing but his arms, his lips, his body against hers.

When he had gone, she knew she could not stay, could never risk being alone with Max again. Always before when the restlessness overcame her, she had forced herself to wind up the loose ends neatly. She had given fair notice to her employers and helped to train her replacement. But this time it was not restlessness, it was fear. She didn't wait for morning. A moment after Max had gone, she was packing what would fit into two suitcases, writing a note to her landlord and slipping it into his mailbox. She didn't go back to work, didn't clean out her desk or pick up her cheque. She ran with the same panic that had been in her heart the day she had finally run away from Ted. Dimly, she realised that it was not Max she was running from, but Ted.

Two hours after Max had closed her apartment door behind him, Lucy was on the freeway outside Toronto, heading north for Sudbury. She reached Sudbury at midday. She found a bank and used her plastic bank card to withdraw money from her Toronto account. She had been receiving a good salary while working for Max, but spending little, so her bank account was healthy enough to support her for a few months if need be.

She turned west at Sudbury, and eventually she was on the Trans-Canada Highway. She spent the next night at a campsite on Lake Superior, sleeping in her car. She was cold and uncomfortable. The following night she slept in a motel on the outskirts of Winnipeg.

Blessedly, her mind seemed to be blanked of all emotion. She continued to drive west. At some point she left the Trans-Canada for the more northern Yellowhead Highway. The Trans-Canada Highway terminated in Vancouver, and she felt Max might search for her in the places where he knew she had lived before.

She drove steadily, stopping only to sleep. On the sixth day she reached the terminus of the Yellowhead Highway, where Prince Rupert was nestled in the hills at the edge of the Pacific Ocean.

Slowly she had built up a life for herself in the coastal community. She had been careful not to give Max any clues of her presence, not to send anyone a change of address. As she had been when she left Ted, she was once again completely isolated from any friends in her past.

The knowledge that Max was now somewhere in Prince Rupert had shaken her so that work was impossible. She had been staring at the program listing for long moments, but thinking of Max. Impatiently, she switched off the power to the computer.

It was two in the morning when she locked the

office door and got into her little red car. The streets were empty. She would be tired in the morning, but right now she was wide awake—wide awake and thinking, remembering a sailboat with a strangely familiar twelve-year-old boy on the deck.

Her apartment would be cold and empty. If she went there, she would spend the rest of the night wondering, worrying.

The docks were silent. When she turned off the engine, the only noise she heard was that of water lapping on rocks. No fishermen on the ramp, no nets on the fingers. A kerosene light flickered dimly through the porthole of one fishboat. Most of the vessels were in darkness.

It was past the hour when sailors visited the neighbours. Most of the boats were empty, their owners gone home. A few had people living aboard, but most of the live aboards were asleep now.

Wanderlust was lying quietly in darkness. Why had she come? What crazy mental arithmetic had she been performing? The boy with the curly brown hair was just a strange boy. It was unlikely that his name was David. It was far too late in the night to go knocking on the hulls of darkened boats.

If she had been startled by the shape of the man who suddenly loomed out of the shadows on *Wanderlust*, she would have gasped. She recognised him at once, but she made no sound, merely stood, silently watching him. He was solid and familiar and all too real.

'Coming aboard, Lucy?'

He gestured to the boarding ladder at the side

of the boat, and Lucy silently slipped her shoes off before she climbed aboard. High heels had no place on those beautiful teak decks.

He led her back to the cockpit, and she made herself comfortable in the corner seat while he disappeared below. She could see his steaming cup on the other side of the cockpit. He had been sitting here, drinking coffee or tea.

She wondered at her own calmness as she waited for Max to return. She had been so shocked by the sight of him that morning that she seemed incapable of surprise now. There was an inevitability about Max being the owner of *Wanderlust*, about the youngster she had seen earlier being Max's son.

He brought her a hot chocolate, as if he had known that she had had her fill of coffee, then he sat across from her and sipped on his own hot drink.

'David told me he talked to a beautiful redhead today. I thought it would be you.'

'We didn't exchange names,' said Lucy. 'Later, I wondered—he looks like you. He has your mannerisms. I didn't know you had a boat like this, otherwise I'd have know he was your son.' The smile was the same. The boy's carefully casual stance was a copy of his father's characteristic pose. His young, earnest face with glints of humour could be a younger Max.

'I bought *Wanderlust* six months ago,' Max told her.

He had talked about a cruising boat that day at the marina, and again on their last night together. He had gone on a three-month cruise to the South Pacific two years before. After that, he had promised himself a yacht of his own when he had built up the business to the point where he could leave it for a while.

'Have you been looking for me?'

She hadn't meant to ask that.

'Yes, I have.' He touched her cheek briefly. 'You must have know I would.'

Yes, she had known. Max could not be evaded by running in the night; he had to be faced directly. 'Why here?' she asked.

'I thought you'd go somewhere near the ocean. You missed the ocean.'

How had he known that about her? She had never told him about her childhood.

'You weren't on the east coast. It's harder to look on the west coast. I looked in Vancouver. You could have been there and I could still have searched and not found you, but I thought you'd go somewhere else. So many of the little towns have no roads, only sea access. This seemed like the best way to look.'

'And now that you've found me?'

It wasn't completely dark. She could see his smile in the moonlight.

'I'll stay around a while.'

'Why? What do you want from me?'

Last time she had run, but there didn't seem much point in running this time.

'I want you to marry me.'

'No!'

She was on her feet, ready to leave when she'd had her say. It was dark and the form on the other side of the cockpit could be anyone. She fancied suddenly that it wasn't Max at all, that it was Ted, taunting her and hurting her, turning her love to terror.

'I'm not going to marry you! I'm not going to marry anybody! Go back to Toronto, Max! There are lots of women there willing and eager to——'

'Stop . . . sit down.' His hand was gentle on her arm. If he had tried to pull her back, she would have fought him, but his voice was as gentle as his hand. The image of Ted faded. She sat, feeling foolish. She knew she had overreacted.

'Relax—I'm not going to force you into anything. Carrying away unwilling damsels went out with the Crusades.'

He was right: Lucy knew that, but she also knew that staying could be dangerous. He was not the only danger; she could be a danger to herself.

'Why did you run away from Toronto?' he demanded.

'Max, I'm not a child. I'm an adult, and if I decide that I want to run away from something—so long as I'm willing to pay the price for running away, I can do that.' The price had been high: Max in her mind through the empty evenings, Ted back in her nightmares.

'Did you run away because I made love to you?'

'Yes.'

'Why?' He was too close now. She could feel his breath on her cheek. His hand was gentle as he turned her face towards his. 'Why, Lucy? It was good for you, too—wasn't it?'

She saw, briefly, a vision of their bodies twisted together in passion. She relived the wild abandon that had possessed her body in the moments before Ted's ghost had forced its way between them.

'Yes,' she whispered, 'it was good for me, too, Max.'

He leaned closer to her and she waited for his lips to touch hers. She knew she should move away, but she was frozen, waiting for his touch. When he gently brushed his lips across hers, the shock was like a pain within her. Her lips trembled until he took them firmly with his own. She shuddered in his arms. Her lips parted to his, and her arms slid around his neck.

He ran his hands up and down her back, sending tremors through her whole body, and she pressed her breasts hard against his chest, knowing she was losing control and not caring.

'Why, Lucy?' His soft voice was insistent against her mouth. He dropped his lips to her neck and she let her head fall back against his arm, glorying in the feel of his lips tracing an erotic pattern on the soft skin of her neck.

'Why did you run?'

'Because I can't handle this.' His lips were still and she could feel the aching in her breasts. She wanted his hands, his lips on her breasts. How could she be wanting him like this? 'I can't handle feeling like this—don't want to want you like this. It terrifies me! I can't handle being vulnerable again. I just can't handle it again.'

'Why? Tell me what happened?'

'No . . . no!'

He stroked her hair as if she were a child. He dried her tears and held her in his arms gently. And Lucy lay quietly in his arms, frightened, yet trusting him.

CHAPTER FOUR

SHE found the note on her desk when she arrived in the morning. She recognised the heavy scrawl of Max's writing upon one of her own internal memo forms.

Lucy,
Will you have lunch with me tomorrow—Friday—at twelve? Your receptionist tells me you have no lunch appointment.
Max

If Cheryl had told Max she was free, she had told the truth. She had an appointment with Dr Fletcher in the morning, and the rest of the day would be spent catching up on the week's work in preparation for Monday. No other appointments.

Max must have left this note for her the day before. He hadn't mentioned it last night, and she hadn't seen it when she was in the office working on the scaling program. She knew that she had no earthly reason for refusing. When she looked at her engagement calendar, she found Max's name written opposite twelve o'clock. Did that indicate that he had impressed Cheryl as a client Lucy would want to encourage? Or did it mean that Max had given Cheryl the idea that there were important personal reasons for the appointment?

It didn't matter. Whatever the reason, she

couldn't avoid this lunch with Max. He had to be dealt with directly. Ignoring him—or trying to—wasn't going to make him go away.

However, dealing with Max was not going to be easy. She had no idea what she could say to him, how she could make him go away.

He wanted to know why she had run away from him. She was terrified of talking about Ted. Max would tell her that she had to get over her fear, that he would help her; but like the person who was terrified of flying, she didn't want to overcome the fear. She just wanted to stay on the ground!

She spent the morning with Max in her mind, not knowing what she would say to him, not knowing how she could handle lunch with him. Overlaying her nervousness was an excitement, a buoyant joy at having Max near again.

Somehow she managed to concentrate on Dr Fletcher when he came for his appointment. At the end of the interview she had accepted another consulting commission. She made an appointment to meet the doctor's office manager at the medical clinic in the middle of the following week, then spent some time alone in her office getting ideas down on paper. Somewhere in the thinking and jotting process, someone had appeared and delivered a cup of coffee to her. She took it with her into the outer office, where Cheryl was just finishing corrections to the mailing list inputs she had done the day before.

Lucy picked up the final print-out of the mailing list and looked it over as she sipped her coffee. Cheryl grinned. 'Are you really going to lunch with the hunk that came in yesterday? He said you'd asked him to make an appointment to discuss his needs. Boy, I wouldn't mind discussing his needs with him! Do you think he needs a blonde?'

Lucy choked on the coffee and had to splutter while Cheryl thumped her back. A client in one of the booths had got up for a cup of coffee and stared curiously at her.

'Cheryl! Hold the sassy comments! I imagine Mr McGraw wants to make some arrangement about the modem. He's pretty sharp, so he probably wants a reduced rate.'

'His name is Max. He told me to call him Max,' drawled the young receptionist in a sultry voice, and Lucy suppressed a grin.

'Well, my name is Boss. So take a letter, slave!'

'Okay.'

Cheryl was willing enough. She listened while Lucy detailed the queries she wanted written.

'You'll find the addresses for all the software houses I mentioned in the address book on my desk. Address the letters to the contact people I've mentioned, then leave them on my desk for signing.'

Cheryl had been making notes furiously, and she seemed to have got it all. She probably wasn't so man-crazy as she seemed; Max had come in and was standing waiting, listening, and Cheryl hadn't batted an eyelash until she'd finished writing.

'Hello, Mr McGraw!' Cheryl smiled enthusiastically at Max, willing him to notice her ripe young body. It occurred to Lucy that Cheryl was dressed to kill today. Dressed for a man, not for the job.

Max nodded acknowledgement, but his eyes hardly flickered as they passed over Cheryl to Lucy. So much for the sultry suggestion that Max had been panting to get on first-name terms! Of course, she had known it was nonsense from the beginning.

'She's deflated,' Lucy told him as they went out. 'She badly wanted you to notice her.'

'She's not deflated,' said Max. 'And what would I do with a young thing like that? By the time she'd bounced around me four or five times I'd be exhausted! I'll stick with older women.'

Lucy giggled. She knew he meant her, but she sensed that he was only joking, with no serious overtones. He was setting the tone of their meeting as light and friendly. She relaxed a little.

'Thanks for numbering me with the middle-aged women! I may be nearing thirty, but that doesn't quite qualify me as an older woman.'

'Older than your secretary!'

'I have a terrible feeling that I never was as young as Cheryl.'

'Here's my car. Hop in!' He held the passenger door open for her.

'We don't need to drive. The Crest Hotel has a nice coffee shop and also a dining room. It's only a block away.' Being alone in the car with him was an intimacy Lucy hoped to avoid.

'I want seafood for lunch,' he told her. 'West Coast crab and real clam chowder.'

She got into the passenger seat. The plastic tag on Max's keys identified the car as a rental.

'If you want good seafood, you have to go to Smiles,' she told him.

'That's what all the tourist guides recommend,'

he agreed. 'And I am a tourist. I've never been to Prince Rupert before.'

'I've been here a year, but I haven't been out to Smiles before.'

'It's about time you went.'

Smiles was smaller than Lucy had thought. There was nothing fancy about the tiny building on the waterfront. Nothing fancy, but the smell of delicious clam chowder, and a menu that promised even greater delights. Max ordered King Crab and Lucy followed suit. It sounded good, and she fancied the crab might have been caught by the large crabbing boat she had seen in the harbour earlier that week.

They shook their heads over the lobster on the menu. Lobster was an east coast dish; no one had yet succeeded in getting lobster to live and breed on the wild western coast of Canada. They agreed that if they were to run the restaurant, they would never have anything on the menu that did not come from the west coast.

As they joked, Lucy relaxed her guard a little. It was good to talk with Max again, now that he wasn't threatening her hard-won peace.

'Tell me about the empire you're building,' he invited her, and she was more than willing.

She described how she had put a notice in the newspaper when she arrived. She described her first client and the mess his books had been in; his gratitude when she straightened out the chaos.

'It was worth it. He was a poor record keeper, but a good talker. I should have paid him for the advertising I got. I never had a chance after that to wonder if I was doing the right thing. Within six months I was so busy I'd had to hire a part-time book-keeper to keep up.

'That was when I started thinking about computers. I had enough revenue to finance one computer system. I applied for a loan at the bank and bought the system and some software—I bought an S.C.S. payroll too.'

'Not in your name, you didn't!' He knew Lucy Carter hadn't so much as phoned S.C.S. since she left.

'No. I ordered it under Do-It-Yourself's name and I paid for it with a money order.' Someone at S.C.S. might have recognised her signature on a cheque, so she'd been careful not to give him a clue like that.

'From there it just mushroomed. A couple of customers were interested in doing their own books on computer, but they didn't want to buy a system. I bought a second system (cash this time) and started renting out Do-It-Yourself computer time. Janice, my part-time book-keeper, went on full time. The demand increased and now I've got two more systems. Most of the time all four are booked solid. I often have to come in at night to get on a computer myself.'

'Is it paying?' Max was a sharp businessman and she was glad of the chance to discuss rates and overheads with him. She told him about her newest developments, Princess Fishery and Dr Fletcher.

'If you're going to get into sales, you'd better nail down an equipment dealership with the manufacturer,' Max advised.

'I'm not sure I want to start selling equipment, Lucy protested.

'There are other alternatives. You don't have to carry any inventory for sale yourself. You could work with a dealer, taking consultation fees and a percentage of sales.'

'That would be better for me. My staff are busy full-time as it is. Sales work would mean new staff, or my doing it myself. If I could turn the actual sales—But, Max, there isn't anyone I know that I could work with that way.'

'Let me think about it for a while, Lucy. I might come up with someone. I have a couple of ideas—I'll have to do some checking. While I'm at it I'll see what I can find out about medical accounting programs for British Columbia. If we can't find anything, we'll write our own.'

'We? Max, you won't be here long enough for that. Don't you have to get back to Toronto?' She tried to suppress the panic that his words roused in her.

'Everything is going fine in Toronto. They can get by without me. Chan is still there, and he knows as much about the payroll program as I do by this time.'

Her breath was short. She could feel the colour coming up in her face and her neck.

'Max, there's no reason for you to stay. I'm not coming back.'

He smiled wryly. 'Don't be dense, Lucy,' he told her gently. 'I'm not going anywhere without you. Now tell me what else you've been doing. Men?'

She shrugged. 'I've been going out a bit.'

'What's his name?'

'John—John Fraser.'

'Serious?' He watched her intently. She didn't answer, but he didn't need an answer. 'No,' he said softly, 'I would know if there were someone serious.'

Would he know? Just how much did he know about her? How much did he guess? And why did he pursue her so relentlessly?

'Come sailing with us tomorrow, Lucy.'

His swift change of subject took her in confusion—or was it a change of subject?

'No! I—why?'

'Because I want you to get to know my son better.'

'Why? What's the point of that?' Lucy had always avoided any of Max's invitations that might result in her being involved in his personal life.

'Because he's part of me.'

She pushed her hands below the table top where he could not see the sudden shaking. Somehow, she must resist him, must stay free.

'I can't, Max.'

What was it that made her feel that she would have no choice but to go with him? The part of her that wanted to go fought a swift battle with her will. She shook her head at him to emphasise her words.

'What are you afraid of?'

She stared at the tablecloth. The waitress set her clam chowder in front of her, and the steam wound slowly up towards her face. She could feel the warm moisture against her skin.

'It's just that I—that I can't ever let myself become that vulnerable again. I couldn't take that again.' She thought of her wedding night, almost ten years ago. She thought of Ted and all the reasons why she could not let herself love Max.

'What was his name?'

'What has that got to do with it? A name is nothing. I've had him in my life enough, I don't need his name floating around the conversation like stale crackers in the soup.' She giggled at the image of Ted consigned to life floating in a bowl of clam chowder, but Max didn't smile.

The silence drew out until she finally realised he would wait for ever for her to say something. She wanted to take a mouthful of soup. She knew she would choke if she did.

'You have to stop pushing me, Max,' she told him.

He nodded.

'Tomorrow? Will you come? No questions about your past—I promise!'

'All right, I'll come.'

Even as she said the words, she knew it was a mistake.

The office was quiet when Lucy returned. Cheryl had gone to lunch, and Janice was in one of the cubicles with a client.

'What if one of the boys on the gas pumps make a mistake?' The client was trying to get the feel of how computerising his company books would work. 'What if Ed writes up a bill to the wrong customer?'

Janice answered patiently.

He had more questions. Janice had answers. He talked; she talked; keys clicked and the computer memory storage disk drives whirred.

A woman came through the front door,

briefcase in hand. Lucy greeted her and waved her on to one of the empty computer booths. A regular client, she made herself at home in the booth and started spreading out papers at the desk beside the computer.

Lucy went into her office and started working on the accumulation of papers on her desk. Janice looked in to say she was going to lunch, then Cheryl looked in to say she was back. Lucy nodded silently to both.

After an hour the pile had been reduced to a few items. She picked up the preliminary print-out of financial statements for Grant's Ladies' Wear. Lucy couldn't approve the financial statements until the bank confirmation arrived. The bank phone line was busy the first time she tried it, so she sorted Dr Fletcher's pile of papers into order before she tried again.

The girl on the switchboard put her through to John Fraser.

'John, it's Lucy.'

'Lucy! I've been trying to get hold of you ever since lunch—I wanted to take you to lunch. What about supper? Dinner at the Crest, then dancing somewhere?'

'I went to lunch with a client.' Did he know she was stalling on the supper invitation? 'I called to ask you to check on something for me.' She gave him the details of the confirmation request she had mailed a week before.

'I'll check into this for you, Lucy. It's probably at the bottom of Steve's in basket.'

'Thanks, John.' He would do it, she knew. She moved the statements back into her basket.

'What about dinner tonight?' he persisted.

'I don't know. I don't really feel like dancing, John—I've had an exhausting week.'

'Lucy, who is Max McGraw?'

How on earth could he know about Max? Who——

'Cheryl said you were out with Max McGraw when I called at lunchtime. Who is he?' John's voice was terse. Jealous?

'Max is a client. I used to work for him in Toronto.'

Cheryl evidently needed a lesson in confidentiality, Lucy thought crossly.

'So you went to lunch?' John was sending disapproval over the telephone line without saying a word.

'Is there some reason I shouldn't?' Lucy bristled at John's assumption that he had a claim.

The silence lasted until his tense voice told her, 'I can't help being jealous of another man, Lucy.'

'You've no right.'

She was being besieged with men. Ridiculous! How many women were there aching for a man, while she seemed to have too many?

'John, I don't belong to you; I don't belong to Max. I'm one of the restless ones. One day I'll leave. I'll move on, and when I do I'll go alone.'

She hung up before he could answer. There was nothing more to say.

Alone.

Her last words echoed in the office.

Alone was best. Friends, yes. John had been a good friend and she would be sorry to lose his friendship, but there was not going to be anything more than friendship. Anything more than friendship left her too vulnerable. No one was going to tear her life apart again.

She admitted to being lonely, but she had been lonely in California, too. Young and lonely and feeling the need for her own people, her own family. When Ted came into her life, he was tall and handsome and masterful. He told her that he loved her, and she told him that she loved him. She met his parents. The wedding banns were called and the sun shone on her as she went into the church in her white dress.

The white had been deserved. Lucy had been a virgin, in spite of the wandering life she had lived. Her parents had been strict in their upbringing and she had grown up with the firm conviction that she must keep herself for the man she married.

For Ted.

She had stood in the church and promised to love and obey him. She had smiled a little about the 'obey' part; it seemed so out of date. But she had known, standing beside Ted in that church, that she would never be alone again. The minister blessed them and Ted kissed her, then they walked out of the church as the organ played.

In a story, they would have lived happily ever after, but Lucy's was no storybook ending. Ted had believed that a wife was a convenience—to cook dinner, keep house, and to be in his bed when the whim took him. What he had taught her of lovemaking had little to do with love, more with pain. Her disillusionment had come quickly. Lucy couldn't be the wife Ted wanted, no matter how hard she tried. Finally, she had realised that life with Ted would never get better. When she escaped, when she regained her freedom, she vowed that no one would ever have that power over her again.

She was glad when the telephone interrupted her memories.

'Lucy, it's John. Look, I'm sorry—I had no right——'

'All right.' If John wanted to stay friendly, it would be more pleasant—as long as he kept the romance to a minimum.

'What about tonight? You said you didn't feel like dancing. How about a trip up Mount Hays in a gondola? Dinner at the top. Look at the view and forget all your troubles?'

If she spent some time with John, it might help her regain her equilibrium. Right now her mind was tied up with Max and with memories of Ted, and a few hours with John might provide a much-needed distraction.

'John, you're a nice man! Yes, all right. I don't promise to be good company, but I'll come.'

Was she crazy? But she couldn't be alone all the time.

When John picked her up at eight that night, Lucy was glad she'd had time for a shower and a half hour relaxing. The meeting with Max had been more upsetting than she wanted to admit. He was far too disturbing to her hard-won tranquillity; yet today she had agreed to yet another meeting.

Max kept burrowing beneath the surface, prying at the reasons for her unwillingness to become involved with him. Could she trust in his promise not to pressure her any more? Probably not. Yet tomorrow his son would be there, too. Surely David's presence would mean that Max would be forced to treat her casually, not to probe or question her?

The shower was hot on her fretful body. Lucy let the water course down her back. She threw back her head and forced everything from her mind except the hot water drumming on her body.

Scrubbed clean, weak from the heat, she dried herself and wrapped her flushed body in the large towel, then she sank down on her bed and picked up the novel from her bedside table. When she had seen the new Helen MacInnes novel on the bookstand she had pounced on it, eager for the fast-paced, gripping tale. Tonight she read slowly, concentrating hard until the drama of the spy story finally took the place of Max in her mind.

When John rang the bell she was ready, dressed in rust-coloured slacks and matching jacket. A soft silk shirt under the jacket clung gently to her body. She looked cool and elegant.

'You look gorgeous!'

Lucy smiled her thanks for the compliment.

'Are we going up in the gondola? Is it open? I've been here a year and I've never been up the mountain.'

'You've been working too hard. You need to relax more.'

That sounded very pleasant and caring. Perhaps she needed that, to be cared for by this gentle man.

'You work hard, too,' she pointed out.

That was true, and John nodded agreement and smiled gently at her.

'We should both relax more.'

They drove through the town in silence. They passed a small park and a large complex, the municipal recreation centre and swimming pool. John turned right and followed a winding road through the trees.

'So different from the city—we were only a couple of minutes away from the wilderness.'

There was no sign of life around them, only the winding road through the trees.

'What city were you thinking of?'

She shook her head with a smile. 'I don't know. Any city. Toronto . . . San Francisco . . . Mexico City . . .'

A large parking lot suddenly appeared ahead. John found a space easily. There were only a few cars at the bottom of the gondola lift. He walked around and opened Lucy's door for her, helping her out with old world courtesy.

'Too many cities,' he murmured above her head. 'What you need is a home.'

It was better if she didn't hear that—or pretended not to. She walked with him towards the building.

'I didn't know they ran the gondola at night. I thought it was only run in the winter for the skiing.'

'It doesn't run every night. When the cruise ships are in the harbour, the gondola usually runs. A lot of the tourists like to ride to the top of the mountain.'

Inside the building, John led her to the loading area where one of the attendants grabbed hold of a gondola as it swept around the curve at the bottom of the lift. He held the door open for them.

They rode up the mountain slowly. John pointed out landmarks—the newest hotel in the city, the airport on the island on the other side of the harbour. Lucy turned and looked and nodded. They got to the top without her disgracing herself by letting anyone see how terrified she was of the swinging journey up the side of the mountain.

She knew the cars were perfectly safe. At least, she told herself they were. At the top, with her feet on the ground again, she was able to admire the spectacular view of the harbour. Instinctively, her eyes went to the harbour entrances. In the south entrance she could see a boat that was probably one of the large coastal ferries. She looked towards the north entrance.

'Just look at that!' She gestured to the panorama below them. 'No wonder that pass is famous. Metlakatla Pass, the north entrance to Prince Rupert harbour. How can anyone navigate that? It's a twisting, tortuous maze.'

'The fishing boats go through it all the time,' John pointed out.

'And some of them run aground, too, don't they?'

He admitted that. 'Once the Pacific Pilot boat even went aground on Devastation Reef. No one was hurt.'

'But it must have been humiliating.' Lucy could imagine how humiliating. The Pilot, the expert who went out to guide foreign ships into the harbour, aground on a local reef!

They turned away from the view and walked to the ski lodge. Upstairs, John led her to a dining room where they sat and enjoyed a warm drink while they looked at their menus.

Their table was at a window overlooking the mountain, the town, the harbour and a vast expanse of ocean. As they watched and talked, the sun set in the western sky. Their dinner came, and they ate as the last red flush faded from the sky. The new moon cast a half light on the vista below.

'You should get out of that apartment you're living in,' John told her as he watched her absorption in the view below. 'You should find someplace else, a nice old place high above the city with a view of the ocean. With all the hills in Rupert, there are many, many places with a view of the harbour.'

She was caught in the mood of the vista below her in the moonlight. She thought of a house high over the harbour.

'Like your place,' she murmured, half to herself. 'Dancing flames in the fireplace and the harbour below. Curled up in an easy chair with a drink, watching the ships go by.'

John missed the note of melancholy in her final words.

'I'll give it to you,' he told her quietly. 'Marry me and it's yours.'

He wanted to say more, but he was afraid to go too far, to say too much. He fell silent and watched her, waiting for her reaction.

Now what had she done? She'd gone off dreaming of a fireplace and a nice view and walked right into the situation she'd been trying to avoid. She wanted to pass it off lightly, but she couldn't think of one casual answer to his offer.

'John, I'm afraid I'm not the marrying kind.'

She sounded like a Western cowboy, insistent on travelling on.

'Are you sure of that? You want a home—you need one. We get along well. I think we could make a good thing of a married life.'

She was glad he hadn't mentioned love.

'John, you would make a good thing of it, but I don't think I would. I've never lived in one place for more than two years in my whole life. I was born wandering and it's in my blood. I'd be a bad risk for you.'

He was shaking his head in denial and she knew he was about to argue. What was she doing? There had to be a better way to say no without being brutal!

'You don't want to wander all your life. If you did, you wouldn't be building a place for yourself here. You wouldn't be starting a business, taking on responsibilities for your clients. Those are all ties that will stop you from moving on easily. Maybe you don't realise it yet, but your subconscious knows that it's time to settle down.'

Lucy knew there was some truth in what he said. But——

'John, let's leave it for now. I'm just not ready to talk about marriage.'

He nodded, picking up their bill. 'Let's go outside and look at the view before we take the gondola down the mountain.'

It could hardly have been more romantic if John had ordered the night. Stars everywhere: she picked out the Big Dipper and Polaris. On board a ship in the middle of the ocean it would be a good night for star sights with a sextant. She wondered if Max meant to cross any oceans in his yacht.

'Beautiful, isn't it?' John had his hand at her waist and she left it there. 'We're lucky to have such a clear night. I think it may be a good summer.'

The weather, did he mean? Or her? She hoped he meant the weather.

Coming down, they rode the gondola back to the real world. As they passed the civic centre they also passed a Royal Canadian Mounted Police car, blue and red lights flashing. An ambulance was just leaving the scene. Someone hurt? Dead? They drove slowly past, not knowing what might have happened.

'Tomorrow,' began John, 'would you like to——'

'No, not tomorrow, John.' He had stopped the car outside her apartment building, and Lucy leaned across and kissed him lightly on the cheek. 'I won't invite you in tonight, John. Thank you for a lovely evening.'

'Goodnight, Lucy.' He returned her kiss solemnly. 'I'll call you.'

CHAPTER FIVE

IN the parking lot the early morning wind gently teased Lucy's auburn curls. She pushed down the button to lock the car door and slammed it. The car was not new and the door had been stubborn about closing lately. She had left her handbag at home—she didn't need money for a day of sailing. Instead, she carried a big beach bag with the odds and ends she thought she might want during the day.

They had agreed on seven as a time for leaving, and she was fifteen minutes early. She slung her bag over her shoulder and started towards the ramp.

The last time she had come to the docks, the ramp had been steeply angled down by the low tide. The range of tides was anything up to twenty-two feet on this part of the North Pacific, and now the ramp was almost flat. Today Lucy was better dressed—jeans and flexible running shoes. Above the jeans she wore a thin, sleeveless blouse covered by a thick wool sweater. The undyed wool of the Aran-knit sweater provided a perfect foil for the red highlights in her hair. She had dressed practically; the thin blouse for hot weather, the sweater in case it was cold.

As she walked along the wharf, she saw that most of the fishing boats were gone. Her shoes made a soft noise on the wooden planks. Ahead, she could see the two masts of *Wanderlust* standing high and proud above the other boats.

She couldn't see the yacht itself yet.

She saw it when she turned up the finger. No one else was stirring, but David was on the wharf, untying one of the lines that secured *Wanderlust*. He smiled at her as she came up.

'I'm not late, am I?' She was fifteen minutes early, but David was casting off the lines and perhaps she had her times wrong.

'You're not late. Dad asked me to take off one set of lines, then it's easier for him to cast off—there's still another set on.'

'Can I help you? I could do the bow.' David looked at her warily and Lucy read his thought easily. 'I do know how,' she assured him.

'Okay,' he agreed.

She dropped her bag on the deck and went forward to the bowlines. She undid the three half-hitches that held the line tied farthest forward on the float. David was watching her. When he decided that she knew what she was doing, he went back and took the line he had loosened on to the stern of the boat. He freed it from the vessel, coiled it and stowed it in the lazarette hatch. Lucy boarded the boat and brought the bowline on board, freed the other end and started coiling it.

'I see he's put you to work already.' Max had come forward from the cockpit. He must have been below when she arrived.

'I have to earn my passage,' she told him. She handed him the coiled rope and he took it from her.

'I can think of other ways you could earn your passage.'

'I'll bet you can!' She laughed because he was smiling, but she could feel his eyes on her and she knew he wanted her.

'There's coffee down below. Bring your bag down and I'll show you where to stow it.'

She followed him into the cockpit where the wheel and navigation equipment were within easy access of the comfortable seats. They went down the companionway steps into the living quarters.

Lucy approved the narrow passage that led forward from the steps. Wide hallways might have aesthetic appeal, but when you were sailing for days on end at sea, you wanted the walls close when you went walking through the boat—you wanted something to grab hold of or to lean against. They passed an open door on the left, showing her a glimpse of a small cabin with a single settee that could serve as a bunk. One side of the cabin was outfitted with computer and disk drive.

'No printer?' Lucy asked Max.

'There are limits to space,' he told her. 'I don't use the printer that often, so it's stowed away. I bring it out and hook it up when I need it. Leave your bag in here. If you need a rest later, you can come down and have a nap.'

'I'm not tired.' She wasn't; she had never been more awake in her life.

They went on into the galley and she saw that the galley counter was almost at the centre of the boat, running fore and aft. That was the best arrangement, she knew—easiest to cook in when seas were rough.

Max reached for the coffeepot on the oil stove in the galley and poured Lucy a cup of coffee. He reached down to open the small refrigerator and pulled out a quart of milk. He had remembered that she liked milk best in her coffee—not cream and not the powdered imitations of cream.

He handed her the cup and she sat at the dinette table across from him. They drank their coffee in silence. In the roomy, comfortable-looking salon, two settees faced each other with a fireplace between. A door led forward to what was probably a sleeping cabin.

'Is that your cabin?' asked Lucy.

'David's. I'm in the after-cabin behind the cockpit.'

'May I look?'

'Of course.'

She took her mug with her and went back. Beside the steps, there was a small passage leading to the after cabin. Along its side, in the curve of the hull, shelves were built in for radio and navigation equipment. Below the shelves was a narrow counter with cupboards below—hatches, she reminded herself. It had been a long time since she had been on a boat like this; but she reminded herself that on a boat cupboards were called hatches, ropes were called lines. She had to bend down to get through the passageway, then she emerged into the after cabin. It was luxurious. A large double berth was surrounded by built-in bookshelves and cabinets. In a corner was a locker for hanging clothes. As in the rest of the boat, walls and ceiling were light-coloured to enhance the feeling of spaciousness, with teak cupboards and teak trim everywhere, giving the warm feeling of elegance and home.

Lucy retraced her steps. Max was still in the galley.

'I have to stow everything before we can sail,' he told her, and she nodded. She knew the chaos that could be caused by dishes left lying about when the boat suddenly heeled far over in response to an unexpected gust of wind.

'I like your yacht,' she told him.

He smiled back at her.

'You'll like her even better when you've sailed her. You've been sailing before?'

Amazing that she had never talked of sailing to him. How could he know so much about her and not know that?

'Yes, I have. I won't scream when you catch the wind in the sails and heel her over.'

'I should have known! Let's go, then. Get yourself a floater vest from the hanging locker in the companionway. I have a rule on board that no one goes up on deck when we're sailing without a life-vest on.'

'It's a good rule,' she agreed, and was glad to find that the vests in his locker were the comfortable Canadian Mustang vests; made to provide warmth and flotation without restricting the limbs. She found a vest that looked like it would fit and pulled it on.

David bounded down the companionway stairs. 'All done, Dad! The ropes are put away. Sorry I was so long, I was talking to the boy on the next boat.'

'Okay, let's go!'

'Can I start the engine?'

Max nodded. 'Be sure it's in neutral before you turn the key.'

'I will.' David went over to the steering wheel and reached down to check the gear shift. Max watched him as he turned the key to one side and held it there. 'It's a glow plug,' David explained to her. 'When I hold the key over to this side, the electricity from the battery goes into the glowplug. When it's hot enough, I can turn the key the other way and the engine will start.'

'How long does it take?' Lucy asked David.

'About thirty seconds. I'm supposed to count to thirty.' Obviously he hadn't been counting this time. He turned the key hard to the other side and the diesel caught at once.

'Rev it up just a bit,' Max instructed David. David reached down and made an adjustment, and Max nodded. 'I'll cast off now.'

He leapt lightly off the yacht. He went to the front and let the rope go. David had run out on deck to pull the rope in as Max let it go from the wharf, and a moment later the aft line was cast off and Max was back on board, spinning the wheel and moving out from the wharf.

They moved gently out from the floats, clearing the log boom that was placed to protect the boats from the waves in the harbour. When they were clear of the boom, David put away the fenders that hung over the side of the boat to protect the hull from banging against the wharf. Max unlashed the sails. Lucy volunteered to handle the steering, and as Max hoisted the first sail, she brought the boat off the wind until she saw the sail fill hard. Max sheeted the sail in and *Wanderlust* sailed off towards the far shore at an angle.

Max spoke and David joined her in the cockpit.

'I'm supposed to shut down the engine,' he told her.

'How do you turn it off?'

'You pull that knob—I'll show you.' He reached past her and pulled hard on a silver knob. As it slid out, the engine sound abruptly ceased.

The woman and the boy stood together in the cockpit, watching the man hoist the second sail, then as the sail pulled tight and filled with wind, they picked up speed. On the starboard side, the water made a whooshing noise as the boat heeled over from the pressure of the wind, and the same wind whipped Lucy's hair around her face.

When all the sails were set, Max joined them in the cockpit. He adjusted the trim of the forward sail with the rope that was cleated down at the side of the cockpit.

'Had breakfast?' he asked Lucy.

She shook her head. She hadn't been hungry this morning. She'd been excited about going sailing, nervous about spending the day with Max.

'We haven't either,' he told her. 'David is cook today.'

'Do you take turns?' Max would teach his son to be self-sufficient, to fend for himself.

David nodded. 'Today I cook and Dad washes dishes. Tomorrow he cooks and I do the clean-up. Would you like bacon and eggs for breakfast?'

'Sounds good. Can I help?'

'Okay.'

'Watch it,' warned Max. 'He'll have you doing it all!'

He didn't, though. David knew his way around the small galley and he soon had bacon in a pan on the stove, bread on a stainless steel contraption that browned four pieces of toast at once. David let Lucy tend to the toast, and soon the aromatic breakfast was on three plates and ready to be eaten.

'We'll eat first,' David told her. 'That's how Dad and I do it when we're sailing. First the cook eats, then the cook steers while the other guy eats.'

'Why don't we all eat in the cockpit this time?' Lucy suggested.

'Well——' David looked so much like his father as he considered her suggestion, 'it isn't too windy. We're riding nice and smooth.' A rough ride could make it hard to hold plates on their laps. 'Okay. Let's take the plates out.'

She and David carried breakfst up to the cockpit.

'It seemed a pity to eat down inside when it's so nice outside,' she told Max. 'We thought we would all eat out here.'

'I appreciate the company,' he smiled at her.

They ate in a companionable silence, listening to the sound of the water on the hull of the boat. Once, Max put down his plate while he adjusted a line to ease one of the sails. When Lucy looked up at him and found his eyes on her, they smiled at each other, and she was suddenly glad that she had come, despite the risks involved in being with Max.

'If we turn off the wind, we should be able to run all the way down the harbour to Metlakatla pass. Take her off, David, and I'll trim the sails.'

David took the wheel and steered the boat around until they had the wind behind them. Max adjusted the sails so they were far out to the side to catch the wind.

'That should be good. It should be fairly easy

to steer on that course. Watch the wheel, David, and I'll clear up the dishes.'

He stacked them quickly and efficiently and started down below.

'I'll help you,' offered Lucy.

He let her come with him, but once they were below he sat her firmly on the settee in the salon.

'You're not helping. You're exhausted and you haven't been sleeping well. Lean back there and watch me work.' He pushed her back and she let herself fall, laughing, against the cushion.

'How do you know I haven't been sleeping well?' It was nice to be lazy. She let her head fall back on to the cushion.

Max had a kettle full of hot water. He was pouring it into the sink, adding cold water and detergent. 'Your eyes,' he answered her.

'Do my eyes tell you that much about me?'

'You'd be surprised how much they tell me.'

It wasn't a comfortable thought—Max seeing through her eyes into her soul. She remembered moments with Max when she had felt he was doing just that, looking into her bare soul.

He was dispatching the dishes quickly and efficently; it seemed no time at all before he had the drainboard stacked with wet dishes. He pulled a dish towel out of a drawer and started drying.

Lucy closed her eyes. She could feel the motion of the boat, gentle and soothing. The last time she had felt that motion had been twelve years ago in the West Indies. The boat, her father's *Lucy Anne*, had been very similar to this boat. She had always loved the process of casting off the lines and moving off on a cruise. Off and away from the world; yet whenever they stopped, they saw a new part of the world, new people.

She felt the soft weight of a blanket dropped over her. She opened drowsy eyes and saw Max's face, Max's eyes looking down at her.

'Go ahead and sleep for a while,' he told her softly. There was something in his eyes that held her own eyes. She remembered the feel of his hands on her body and knew he could see her remembering. He bent down and brushed her forehead with his lips, then he moved away from her and she managed to keep herself from calling out for him to stay, closed her eyes again and kept herself from saying his name until he had gone back up on deck.

Why did Max always have this effect on her? Something in him called to her, and when he came near her she wanted things that she had not wanted for a long time. But it wouldn't work—couldn't work. She had to remember that.

Remember . . . she remembered only too well the night that Max had taken her out in Toronto. The night she had invited him in for coffee.

Max had leaned against the wall while she searched for her keys outside that apartment in Toronto. She had found them and opened the door.

He stood there still, his eyes telling her what he was waiting for.

'Max——'

'Are you going to invite me in?'

She didn't know if it was excitement or fear that caused her heart to pound so hard in her chest. She had looked up at him, unable to speak. When she went into the apartment he followed her through the door and closed it for her.

Suddenly nervous, she left him in the living room while she went into the kitchen. She filled a kettle and placed it on the stove to boil, then reached into a cupboard for coffee. She sensed Max's presence behind her and her hand froze, reaching for the coffee tin. His fingers touched the bare skin of her arm. He moved his palms softly along her trembling skin to her hands; then bent and placed his lips gently on her neck, so bemusing her that when he tugged on her hand she let him lead her into her darkened sitting room.

He led her over to the big, overstuffed antique that was her favourite chair. As he sat, he pulled her down on to him until she was lying across him, her head and shoulders cradled in the soft curve of the chair back.

Their faces were close together, and even in the shadows she could see the caress in his eyes as they touched her lips, her neck, the swelling of her breasts. An unfamiliar passion stirred in her, responding to the desire in his eyes.

When she thought she would die of the waiting, Max bent to her. His lips brushed gently against hers until her eyes had to close from the light in his. He ran his tongue along the underside of her upper lip, and her head fell back and her lips parted. Somewhere deep inside her, Lucy watched herself as she lay pressed against Max, inviting him to kiss her more deeply.

His hands caressed her skin through the thin fabric of her blouse, stirring a longing she had never expected to feel. Then he raised his head and the room was silent as he slowly opened her blouse. He found the front fastening on her bra and freed her swelling breasts from their confinement.

His whisper was hoarse with emotion.

'Lucy—I knew you would be beautiful.'

His hands cupped her breasts and he bent his head to one, licking the hardened nipple gently. She groaned aloud as his tongue moved. As he took the aroused tip of her breast deeply into his mouth, she shuddered, her arms reaching up, her fingers tangling in his hair, holding him tightly. She arched against him, pressing her body close, straining and twisting against him as his hands, his lips, his tongue caressed her soft white body.

When the fever of her passion had become almost unbearable, when his caresses had become a torment too sweet to bear, he lifted her and laid her down on the carpet. As he bent to kiss her, his hand caressed the roundness of her stomach and the quivering, aching place that was her thighs and the very heart of her passion.

She hardly knew when he gently removed her slacks, running his hands softly, teasingly down her hips as the fabric slid away from her.

Then his hands left her, and she felt the coolness of the night air on her thighs and her breasts as Max undid the buttons of his shirt, undid his belt.

His shadow loomed as he lowered his body over her.

Lucy could hear the kettle boiling in her kitchen; she could hear the creaking of the elevator in the hallway outside the apartment.

Above her, she could see the looming shadow

of Ted. Not Max making love to her; but Ted looming, threatening.

Her blood chilled. The passion died and she lay shivering in the night air. Max reached his hands down and caressed her cold, empty body.

'Lucy?' His whisper hardly touched the surface of her memories.

'Go away . . . leave me alone.' Her eyes were blank so that he felt she was not even there in the room with him.

When he had gone, she lay shivering for a long time. Then she got up, dressed, and started packing her possessions.

CHAPTER SIX

THE change in sound wakened Lucy. She knew where she was at once when she opened her eyes—on a boat, Max's boat. She had wakened with the alert knowledge of the sailor. Something had happened, some change.

She felt the vibration of the diesel engine and knew what had wakened her. They were no longer travelling under sail. The engine had been started. She got up and folded the blanket Max had placed over her earlier. She had no idea where it was normally stored. She laid it on the settee where she had slept, then she went into the bathroom—or head, as it was properly called—and splashed cold water on her face to drive away the groggy feeling. When she had found her comb and put her curls in order she felt ready to face the world.

She was just starting to climb up the stairs when Max called down to her.

'Don't get between me and the depth-sounder!'

She craned her neck to locate the display that gave Max a constant reading of the depth, then ducked and came up into the cockpit. He was obviously intent on the depth-sounder, the navigation chart, and the terrain around. David was standing at the back of the cockpit, well out of Max's way. He grinned at Lucy as she came up, but he was silent.

She stood beside David and looked around.

The sails were still up, but they were lashed to the centre of the ship. The wind flapped them at times, but there was no steady wind in this narrow, protected passage. She could make out a navigation light ahead on the shore, and a marker on the shore behind them. Max was running *Wanderlust* on a line between the two, but he would have to change course soon. Ahead, the passage made a sharp turn to their left. Lucy moved a little so that she could see the chart in front of Max. She studied it silently. Max was glancing to his left frequently as they came abreast of the turn in the channel, then he swung the ship until she was heading directly for a floating back buoy. Lucy could see that some of the tension in him had gone, although he was still alert and careful. She was glad to see that he was not the casual kind of sailor who risks his ship and his life with little thought for the consequences.

He glanced down at her.

'Sorry if I shouted at you. We're out of the shallow area for the moment.' He watched her glance at the chart. 'Do you know where we are?'

She pointed to a spot on the chart. 'Just here, I think. We've just come through that shallow leg of the channel—it looks like you can only go through at high tide. Those houses up ahead should be Metlakatla village. Are you heading for this can buoy now?' she pointed to a mark on the chart.

'You didn't place us that accurately without a lot of experience of marine chart navigation.' Max had time now to glance down at her searchingly.

Of course she had a lot of experience, years of it, but by force of habit she changed the subject. Since leaving California she hadn't talked of the past to anyone. She had tried to pretend that there was no past.

'Are we going to stop at the village?' she asked him. She tried to see details of the houses ahead, but it was too far. David handed her a pair of binoculars and she focused them on the houses. She could make out a dock and the red rails on the ramp down to the wharf. Those red rails usually indicated that the wharf was a public facility installed by the government.

'I hadn't planned to stop,' Max told her. 'Once we get through this pass we'll be in Chatham Sound and we could have a good sail across to Lucy Island Lighthouse—you shouldn't miss the chance to see the island that has your name.'

'Yes, let's!' She was aching to feel a wild, sailing ride; the hull heeled hard over and the noisy rush of water as the vessel strained with the wind. It was windy enough here in the sheltered parts that Chatham Sound should give them a good ride.

'Lucy?' Max's voice was quiet behind her. 'Lucy, you can't spend your life mourning for a lost love. You have to get on with life. There's no point in being faithful to a memory for ever.'

A lost love. Max thought she was unwilling to be unfaithful to the man she had loved. He had added up the evidence, but he had it wrong. He'd come up with an old love who had taken her sailing, a secret love she would not betray.

Perhaps it was better if he thought that. Hard to fight a ghost.

This day with Max was cheating. She knew she

had nothing to give him, could have nothing to give him. Spending time with Max and his son was going to give him the wrong impression. When this day was over, that would have to be the end of it. The longer it went on, the worse the ending would hurt. It was tempting to take Max at face value; to let him help her with her problems at Do-It-Yourself; to let him take her to lunch and sailing. It seemed so easy to say that they could be together as just friends, but that night in Toronto had changed everything. The memory of that night was in Max's eyes and in her mind whenever they were together.

She turned away from Max and handed the binoculars back to David.

'Do you see the village?' she asked the boy.

He nodded. 'I saw fields, too, behind the village. It looks like there are fruit trees in the hills behind the village.'

Max agreed. 'The whole area looks like it was cleared at one time. The growth is very different around the village, not the dark evergreen growth that's usual on this coast.'

'Do you think there are apple trees and orange trees?' asked David.

'Apples, maybe,' said his father. 'And pears and plums. Not oranges, it's not hot enough in this area to grow oranges.'

'The village looks nice, doesn't it?' murmured Max. 'So many of the houses are painted in bright colours.'

'It's a fishing village,' Lucy told him. 'Most of the native families have a fishing boat or work on a relative's boat. I wonder why there aren't any boats at that wharf.'

'Salmon opening,' Max told her. 'Department of Fisheries opened salmon in Chatham Sound at four o'clock this morning, and all the boats went out last night.'

Lucy eyed the empty docks. What did the women do while the men were out fishing? What was it like when the boats came in? All the women would be down to meet the men. The wharf would be crowded with boats and men and their families and their dogs.

She watched the shore as they passed the village. It was a small village. There was a boy riding down the road on a bike, another child playing on the wharf with two dogs. Three women stood by a fence, talking. No men.

When they were through the pass, the white fishing boats out on Chatham Sound seemed to fill the horizon. The sails of *Wanderlust* made a popping noise as the first gust of wind from the sound hit them.

'A north wind,' said Max. 'We'll have a beautiful sail to the island. See the light ahead?' He started loosening the ropes to adjust the sails.

The light was several miles ahead and Lucy couldn't see it yet. Max was right about the wind. The north wind blew hard enough to give Lucy the ride she wanted. Their worst problem was the fishing boats with their nets.

'Lucky it's a beam wind,' muttered Max. 'We would have trouble steering our way through this sea of nets and fishing boats on any other course. Actually, we could run over their nets without doing any damage—our propeller isn't spinning now that the engine is shut down; but I've found that a lot of the fishermen don't know that a sailboat under sail is no danger to the nets. I'd rather take the few extra minutes to steer our way around them.'

As they sailed further into the Sound, they found that there were fewer nets in their path. Max set the sails to make a good course towards the island.

'That looks pretty stable. Watch the steering while I go down to make some coffee for us.'

'Can I come, too?' asked David. 'Can I get a glass of juice?'

Max hesitated, looking at Lucy.

'Go ahead,' she urged him. 'It's all right with me. I won't steer you into any rocks. If I get into trouble, I'll shout loud enough.'

The hazardous rocks were all behind them now.

She checked the sails and made a careful note of the spot on the horizon they were sailing towards. She confirmed their location on the chart, then checked the reading on the compass. In case of sudden fog, it was essential to know what course to steer on the compass.

She went through this routine without thought, following habits instilled in her as a child. Once she knew everything was shipshape, she leaned back and enjoyed her solitude.

She was very aware of Max below decks. She could hear only the sounds of the ocean on the hull, but if she called she knew he would come to her. The wind was steady in the sails, but they would sail only two or three more miles before they would have to change course. The clouds to the west could turn threatening. The wind could blow up into a gale on a day like this.

Certainly this vessel could ride out a gale. So could her owner, Lucy was sure. Max was neither foolhardy nor easily frightened. Lucy and her family had travelled the oceans, meeting many other vessels with many other skippers. She had learned early how to judge a good sailor. She had met many good sailors; she had also met many that she would never consent to travel with.

She knew that she could safely go anywhere in the world in a vessel skippered by Max; that Max would ask her to come with him. It was that knowledge that gave her the tightness in her throat, the tense wariness that was keeping her on edge today.

As they sailed out into the sound, the wind was shifting more towards their head. The angle of the sails was no longer the most efficient for the wind direction. Lucy shifted course slightly to make for the south end of Lucy Island. Automatically, she made the adjustments to trim the sails for the new course. She found the winch handle and used the lower speed on the winch to pull the jib tight against the wind.

They were sailing hard now, heeled over with the sails close-hauled. She hoped that Max wasn't having any trouble using the stove at this angle of heel, but suspected that everything below was well outfitted for cooking under sail. She smiled at him when he appeared in the cockpit with a cup for each of them.

'Where's David?' The wind had whipped her hair until it was a riot of curls around her head, and her cheeks were flushed from the wind and the excitement.

'Down below. He got into a book while I was

boiling the water, and fell asleep on the settee, reading.' Max's eyes noted the change in the set of the sails. He'd heard the winch from down below, so he knew she had been busy.

'You should have called me to set that mainsail,' he said. 'I don't want you to hurt yourself.'

'I didn't. I took it into the wind until I had the line cleated tight, then I brought it back. That's the lazy man's way.' She was standing at the wheel. When Max handed her the cup she moved aside and let him take the wheel. The sails were set so that the boat was virtually steering herself.

They stood side by side in the cockpit, not needing to speak. Lucy felt an intense awareness of Max's presence which she knew he shared. For a time, crossing Chatham Sound, they were the only two people in the world.

They lost most of their wind as they passed the end of Lucy Island. Max took down the sails and started the engine again. He dropped the anchor, then had Lucy shift the engine into reverse and go full astern to be sure that they were solidly anchored.

When the engine was off again, they sat silently on the deck, listening to the sound of wind in the trees and the lapping of water on the hull.

'You're pretty good at this sailing business,' Max spoke quietly. David was below, still sleeping. If he had been awake he would surely have come up to see their anchorage.

It was a beautiful spot. They had anchored in a bay on the far side of the island from the lighthouse. On shore, a great expanse of sand surrounded the bay, good beach for walking or playing. It would have been a good beach for swimming, but the water in the North Pacific was too cold for swimming, even in summer.

'It's a long time since I've been sailing,' Lucy told Max at last. 'It's been twelve years—not since I was fifteen years old.'

Overhead, a bald eagle circled, looking for prey. The magnificent bird glided in a huge circle, his wings motionless. Then, with one forceful pump of his wings, he angled up and over the trees on the shore. Max leaned back on deck, his empty coffee cup in his hands.

'Tell me,' he said.

'I was born wandering,' she told him. 'My father loved the sea. He was brought up in a seaside town in England. He watched the ships while he grew up, but his family were farmers—rich farmers—and he was supposed to be a farmer as well.

'Dad used to haunt the docks, talking to the people on the boats that came in. Most of them were fishing boats, but sometimes a sailboat would arrive. In those days there were not so many people cruising the world in sailboats, but when Dad was seventeen a big one came in. They were rich people with a hired crew to do the work of sailing. One of the sailors left them there, and they asked Dad if he wanted to crew for them.

'Dad went home and packed a bag. My grandmother tried to stop him, but the sea was in his blood already. He was two years on that boat, then he found a job on shore and started working to buy his own boat. He began writing about some of his experiences at sea. He sold the odd story, and he had the idea that if he could manage to get his own boat, he might pay his way around the world with his writing.

'By the time he was twenty-five he'd managed to buy a thirty-foot sailboat. He outfitted it and got a bit of money ahead, then he went cruising. He sold some of his writing. For the rest, he worked at odd jobs here and there.

'He was twenty-seven when he first cruised up the California coast. He was no lover of big cities, but he had some extensive engine repairs to have done and he stopped for several months on the California coast.

'My mother was there, working in the office of the marina where he had tied up. Dad always said he knew he would marry her the first moment he saw her. Her family liked Dad, but they didn't approve of her going wandering around the world with him. Mom's sister tried everything she could to stop them; however, when the engine was fixed, Mom and Dad were married and they went cruising.

'I don't know if she wanted that kind of life, but it was Dad's life and she went with him. After I was born, they bought a bigger boat. Mother's name was Anne, and he named the boat for both of us—the *Lucy Anne*.

'Sometimes we cruised for months without stopping for more than a day or two in any one place. Occasionally, we stopped for a few months or a year. Whenever we stopped for more than a few weeks, Mom would take me to the local school. Usually they didn't know what to make of my weird educational background. In between, I worked on correspondence lessons. By the time I was twelve I could speak English, Spanish,

French, and a little German, and I knew something about the customs of a dozen different countries. I knew how to rig a sail, and how to scrape and paint anti-fouling paint on the bottom of a boat.

'I didn't know how to ride a bicycle—even riding in a car was an unusual event for me. After my twelfth birthday things changed a little. Dad had written a book that was published the year I turned twelve, and suddenly we found that when we came into port, word would have come ahead of us. We were often met by people who'd read Dad's book. We were invited to homes, taken on outings. By the time I was fifteen Dad had published a second book and it was doing even better than the first.

'We spent that year in the West Indies. Mom was worried about my education, so she registered me in a private school in St. George's in the Caribbean. I made friends at school and started leading quite a social life that year. It was the first time I'd had my own social life—we'd always done things together as a family. Our home was the boat, but that could be anywhere in the world. Our neighbours were always changing, although we often met the same people again and again in different parts of the world. That year in St. George's was different. I think Mom and Dad were beginning to realise I was growing up and to wonder what they should do about me.

'One weekend I was invited to stay with a friend's family. Betty, a girl from school, had invited me to her home for a holiday weekend. On Saturday the wind began to blow. It was no ordinary wind.

'Mom and Dad were anchored in the harbour when the storm hit. It was hurricane season, but no one had predicted that this storm would come anywhere near us. If they had known, they would have put to sea where the boat could ride out the strong wind. In the harbour they didn't have a chance. They were smashed on the rocks. Their bodies were never found, but everyone knew they couldn't have survived in the water that night.'

Below, the sound of a cupboard opening intruded in the stillness. David was stirring. Max turned his mug in his hands, then set it aside.

'Barry Jamieson,' he murmured.

'Yes,' she nodded, 'that was my father. Have you read his books?'

'I have them on board—about him and his wife and their daughter Lucy sailing on the *Lucy Anne*. I read them, but I never connected them with you. The girl in those books was Lucy Jamieson, not Lucy Carter.'

He reached across to her and tucked a stray curl behind her ear. She watched a flock of seagulls circling at the far side of the bay.

'What happened then, Lucy?' His voice was soft, deceptively soft. 'You were fifteen, alone in the Caribbean, orphaned. What then?'

'I was on my mother's American passport, so the Consulate sent me back to the States—to my mother's sister.'

'And her name wouldn't have been Carter?'

'No.' Lucy didn't want to talk about the rest of it. He was waiting for her to talk, but she wasn't ready.

'My name changed because I got married.' Her words echoed in the bay, harsh in the silence. 'I don't want to talk about that—I'm not ready to talk about my marriage.'

'When will you be ready?' asked Max.

'Maybe never—probably never.' Telling Max about Ted could leave her defenceless, and she had so few defences against Max as it was. All the unspoken words swirled between them there on the deck of *Wanderlust*. Lucy pushed herself to her feet and faced him defiantly.

'Are we going ashore here?'

Max nodded, then he stood and took her cup from her. 'I thought we might light a fire on the beach and have a wiener roast. David would like that.'

She heaved a silent sigh of relief. Max had dropped the inquisition, although a glance at his face told her it was only a temporary respite.

Max rowed David and Lucy to shore with strong, easy pulls on the oars. David insisted on carrying their lunch supplies in a packsack on his back.

'I'll start the fire,' he told Lucy. 'Dad taught me how to start a campfire and he always lets me do it now. Can I roast your wiener for you?'

'Sure,' agreed Lucy. 'I always seem to burn them. I like my wieners a nice golden brown, but they never come out that way for me.'

'I'll get them right for you,' David assured her. 'Dad, once I get the fire started, can I go looking for sea-urchins in that rocky bay over there?'

'First we should try to find the lighthouse-keeper,' Max told him. 'As far as I can make out from the chart, this whole island is government property, so we should get permission before we start lighting fires.'

Beyond the sandy expanse of beach they could see a large wooden structure that supported a helicopter pad.

'The Sikorsky helicopter lands there,' David told them excitedly. 'All the lighthouses have big helicopter pads, so the Sikorsky can land there. I met one of the pilots at the floats in Rupert, and he said they bring most of the groceries out, and at Christmas they bring Santa Claus around to all the lighthouses—for the little kids who still believe in Santa,' he added.

'If they land the groceries on that pad, there must be a path or boardwalk to the houses,' speculated Max.

They found the boardwalk above the high tide line of the beach. Soon they were walking along the wooden walk among tall evergreen trees, out of sight of the ocean. Occasionally they heard a bird thrashing through the branches.

'Strange,' whispered Lucy. 'We could be miles from the ocean, lost in the woods.'

'We'll get to the houses soon,' David reassured her. 'The island is only a mile long.' He moved up beside her to offer his support.

'Right around the corner,' said Max, 'I think I hear a dog barking.'

'A big dog,' warned Lucy.

The dog was probably part St Bernard; certainly he was big enough. The three intruders stopped to let the dog approach them. He growled a little as he came up to them.

'I've never heard of anyone being bitten by a St Bernard,' whispered Lucy. 'They're supposed to rescue lost mountain climbers in the Swiss Alps.'

'He's not going to bite us—are you, fellow?' Max held out a hand to the dog. 'Just doing your job, aren't you? Keeping strangers in line.'

The dog ambled over and sniffed his palm, then turned and walked along with him.

'I must be using the right kind of after-shave lotion,' grinned Max.

'Whatever it is, I hope you don't lose it,' murmured Lucy. 'As long as he's around, I'm sticking close to you!'

Max laughed. 'I've been looking for a way to keep you close. Now I've found it.'

The girl who came out of the house ahead of them took their breath away. She was tall and slender with alabaster skin and long black hair. She ran down the stairs towards them, her glossy black hair flying behind her.

'Hi! I'm Bobby Drake! Isn't it a lovely day?' The dog came over to her and pushed his massive head against her hand. She stroked him absently. 'This is Barney, our watchdog—actually he's a real teddy bear, but we don't usually tell people that.'

'He kept us in line,' Max told her. 'I'm Max McGraw, and this is Lucy—and David. We were out sailing and anchored in your bay for lunch. We wondered if anyone would mind if we lit a campfire there.'

'No problem, as long as you put out the fire when you're done and take away your garbage.' The girl turned to David. 'Are you interested in seeing some livestock? We've got chickens and goats! My nephew is just feeding the chickens.'

'Sure! Where is it?' David was all set to go as

soon as the animals were mentioned. The dark-haired beauty pointed towards a small building on the hill behind the houses. David looked at his father for permission, then ran off towards the chicken house. Barney, the dog, went with him.

'Maybe you'd like to see over the station while you're up here,' Bobby Drake invited Max. 'My brother is painting the light-tower—I'm sure he'd enjoy a break to show you around.'

'That's an offer I can't refuse,' smiled Max. An offer? wondered Lucy. Or a woman? 'You have a beautiful place here.'

'It isn't really mine. I'm visiting my brother for the summer. This is a good place to sit back and try to figure out what comes next. I'm trying to decide whether to go back to university next year, or to start trying to support myself. Meanwhile, I'm sitting on Lucy Island for the summer, watching the fish and the boats go by.'

Bobby smiled at Max again. Lucy moved closer and slipped her hand into the crook of Max's arm, smiling determinedly at Bobby.

'I think we would like to see the station, if your brother wouldn't mind.'

'Okay. I'll just get my jacket—it's windy going across to the lighthouse.'

Bobby disappeared into the house and Max slipped his arm free of Lucy's hand, putting it around her waist to guide her further down the boardwalk.

'What was that for?' he murmured in her ear 'Jealousy?'

Lucy's face flamed. 'I'm sorry—I don't know why I did that.'

He laughed. 'You certainly gave her the "No

Trespassing" signal! She probably didn't need it. I imagine she thinks we're married.'

Of course, she would. A couple arriving with a young boy. The basic family unit—mother and father and son.

They walked past the two houses to the bridge that spanned a chasm between the residences and the lighthouse tower. Lucy leaned against the rail of the bridge and looked down at the water swirling in the chasm below. They had come to the other end of the island now.

'It's beautiful,' she murmured. 'A beautiful place to live, but——'

'Not for a restless girl like you,' agreed Max. 'You need a little more variety in your life than can be had on a lighthouse.' He looked back towards the houses. 'For that matter, so do I. A fascinating place to visit, but——'

'But I wouldn't want to live here,' concluded Lucy. 'I wonder if she would—Bobby?'

'Oh, I think she might not mind the life here. She looks like a witch, but I think she wants to raise babies and put down preserves in the pantry. Not your style, Lucy.'

'I can do those things.' Illogically, she resented his assumption that she was incapable of the fine art of housekeeping.

'Have you ever raised babies?' he asked.

'No. No, I haven't.'

'Would you like to?' He was close to her now, so close.

Her breath was short. She moved a step away. 'I don't know.'

She had let this conversation get far out of hand. She should start talking about the weather or the buildings around them, anything but herself and Max.

'Max?' she queried.

'Hmm?'

'What was David's mother like?'

'It was a long time ago, Lucy. I don't know how accurate my memory is.' He took her hand in his and they stood together, leaning on the rail. 'We were both very young. She was tall, and dark, a nice-looking girl. I guess we were in love—or thought we were.

'We had David just a year after we married. When David was two, she took him with her shopping one day. There was a pile-up on the freeway and she was killed instantly. David was badly hurt.'

'Does David remember her?'

'He has a picture that I gave him, but I don't think he has any real memories of his mother.'

Lucy thought of the boy growing up without a mother. Max had obviously done a good job in bringing up David, but it couldn't have been easy.

'Was she pretty?' she asked.

'I guess so.' He rubbed his thumb across the back of her hand. 'I know I thought so then. We were happy enough at the time. We didn't fight, didn't have any big problems that I remember.' He released her hand to draw his fingers gently across her cheek. 'It was ten years ago, Lucy. I was a different person then. I know I never felt the depth of feeling that I have for you.'

His words sent her heart pounding hard against her ribcage. His eyes repeated what his lips had said and her own eyes were trapped, returning a message to him, one that she hadn't wanted to send.

Max dropped his hand. 'Here's our escort. Smile and be nice to her.' He was still amused by her display of possessiveness earlier. What had got into her? she wondered. If she wanted Max to leave her alone, she had no right to post a claim on him.

Tom Drake was halfway up the side of the lighthouse tower, suspended from a rope that was attached to the top rail of the tower. He had a paint sprayer in his hand, and the roar of a compressor engine from below him. Bobby shouted to her brother, but he didn't hear.

'Would you like to come to the house for a cup of coffee after you've seen around the station?' asked the dark-haired girl.

Max shook his head. 'I've promised my son a wiener roast for lunch, and we're hoping to go on to Hunt's Inlet for the night.'

'I'll run up and get Tom, then.'

'Don't bother him,' said Max. 'Let him get on with the job. We can tour round the buildings another time.'

'No bother!' She was gone through the door into the tower before Max could protest again. She must have run up the circular stairs inside; it was only seconds later that her head appeared over the rail and she waved her arms at the man with the paint sprayer.

'I'd hate to think that she'd startle him like that. What if he fell?' Lucy could easily visualise the man crashing to the cement below.

Max didn't share her concern. 'He's well

secured. He's sitting in a bosun's chair and he has a safety rope as well.'

They moved a few steps away from the noisy compressor. 'It's something I've never got used to.' Lucy made a face at the high tower. 'Whenever Dad had to be hoisted up the mast, I was always certain he would come crashing down to the deck and be killed. He was always well secured, too, but——'

'Didn't your seagoing training include a course in climbing tall masts?'

'I guess I missed out on that part,' she confessed. 'Dad always did the climbing. I've never had a head for heights—frankly, I'm terrified at the thought of going on a ferris wheel or a gondola.'

'The girl who doesn't hesitate to cross an ocean in a small sailboat, terrified to go on a ferris wheel!' he grinned.

'It's crazy, I know—not logical at all!'

'Fears are seldom logical. You needn't worry, I'll climb your masts for you.'

No, he wouldn't. Right now was not the time to tell him, but this day was the last day they would have. Spending this day with Max was probably a mistake, but she was here now. She would enjoy it while it lasted.

She watched as Tom Drake began to lower himself slowly down the side of the tower. Max stood beside her, watching along with her.

'I didn't know we were planning to go on to Hunt's Inlet for the night.' Lucy was careful to keep her voice toneless.

Max didn't look away from the man on the tower. 'It's a pleasant place to visit—a little community of houses in an isolated bay. Most of the houses are deserted, just summer cottages. We could sail there in a few hours, be in before dark. Low tide will be about nine tonight. We could dig some clams on the beach, let them soak overnight, then have clam chowder tomorrow while we have a leisurely sail home to Rupert.'

'You didn't mention staying out overnight when you asked me.'

He turned towards her then. 'What are you afraid of, Lucy? Rape isn't my style—and you're far from helpless! You're capable of dealing me a painful kick if I get out of line. If that doesn't work, there's this twelve-year-old chaperon—David! All you have to do is call out and any intimate moment will end instantly.'

Tom Drake had almost reached the bottom of the tower when Bobby emerged from the structure and ran over to them.

'I'll leave you with Tom,' she said. 'I've got to check that my nephew is feeding the chickens the right mix. You can pick your son up at the chicken house on the way back—if you're sure you won't stay for coffee?' She directed the question to Lucy this time, but again it was Max who answered.

'Thanks, but I'm afraid we can't.'

'Another time, then? Next time you come, my sister-in-law may be here. She's in town waiting to give birth to her baby right now, she should be back in about a month.'

'Another time,' agreed Lucy, knowing it would never happen. She had got over her insane surge of possessive jealousy and was beginning to think that Bobby Drake might be worth knowing better. When Bobby turned in the middle of the bridge to wave, Lucy waved back to her.

Max had moved away to talk to the lighthouse keeper. The noisy compressor had stopped and Lucy could hear their words now.

'I'm here alone at the moment. Usually there are two of us—the senior keeper and me, but Saul is away on holiday right now, so I'm alone. My wife is away, too. Marlene would have loved the company! She's expecting our baby any day now. My young lad is excited at the prospect. He's eleven and I think he's planning to be the one who brings up the new baby. Roberta's excited too. She gave up her summer job and came out to help, and to spoil the new baby when it comes.' The paint-spattered man grinned, 'Hell, I'm excited, too! We've been trying to give Andy a sister for years. For us, this is the event of the decade!—What do you want to see? Want to climb up the tower and see the view?'

'Sounds good, if you can spare the time.' Max quirked his eyebrows at Lucy. 'I think Lucy would rather wait at the bottom.'

'I'll come.' She was afraid of heights, but she wasn't missing the tour because of that.

She climbed the stairs carefully. At the top, Tom swung across the open exit in a manner that suggested he might be trying out for the part of Tarzan. Max followed his lead easily, but turned back to offer his hand to Lucy. The gap between the top of the stairs and the landing was about two and a half feet; on land she would have thought nothing of it. She locked her eyes on Max's hand and refused to look down. When she was halfway across the gap he caught her waist firmly with his free hand. When she was on the platform she closed her eyes for a moment, pretending she was on the ground. Then she looked carefully for her footing and moved out of his arms.

'Okay?' he asked her.

She grimaced. 'I'll survive it. This platform is really quite secure.'

'It is,' he agreed. There was a double rail around it. Unless she was insane enough to throw herself over the rail, the only danger was in her imagination.

Tom pointed out the landmarks, and Lucy agreed that the view was fabulous. She looked back towards the bay where *Wanderlust* was anchored, but the hill behind them obscured the view. When Tom Drake turned to take them back down, Lucy went first. Years ago she had learned that the scariest part of her fears was waiting for her turn. If she went first, it was over quickly.

Back at ground level, Tom led Max and Lucy towards the engine room. Lucy followed behind the men. In the noisy engine room, she couldn't hear them talking. She watched their lips as Max asked questions and Tom answered. She was storing up memories of Max, but she probably had all the memories she could handle. Leaving Toronto had been painful, but this parting would be even worse.

The notion flitted across her mind that she did not have to drive Max away; that she could give in to his pursuit of her. As the idea settled in her mind, she felt again the pain of the ultimate loneliness—the pain of loving and wanting love; of living the fantasy of love and waking up to the reality of loneliness. Never again would she open herself to that pain. Choosing to be alone was better than the betrayal of love.

When they came out of the engine room, the natural sound of water on rocks was a welcome relief to her ears. They said goodbye to the lighthouse keeper and crossed the bridge to collect an exuberant David.

'He's taking school by correspondence, too,' David informed them. 'He gets his lessons from Victoria, though. I get mine from Ottawa.'

'Different provinces,' said Max. 'I arranged for your correspondence lessons before we left Toronto.'

'Well, his lessons seem about the same as mine. He's ahead a year. He worked five hours a day at first, but now that he's got so far ahead, his mom and dad let him just work mornings on schoolwork.' David looked pointedly at his dad.

'If you get that far ahead, we'll discuss it.' The look on his father's face told David there was no point in arguing that point.

'Well, they have quite a time here. In the winter the wind blows hard, sometimes they're cut off for days on end. The helicopters can't land if the wind is too strong. They get all their groceries by helicopter or by ship. When the ship brings the groceries, they lift it up on to the platform from the ship's workboat. Andy says he's learning to run the hoist that lifts the groceries. His mom likes it better when the helicopter comes—too many eggs get broken when the groceries come by ship. They only get their groceries once a month! Can you imagine that?'

'Lucy should be able to imagine it,' commented Max.

She nodded. 'My family would stock up for two to three months when we crossed the ocean.'

'Wow! Did you ever cross the Atlantic? I hear it gets rough!'

'Sometimes it does. We always crossed when the winds were most favourable, so we avoided the storms.' Lucy could see that David was disappointed at what he viewed as overtly tame ocean crossings.

They found driftwood above the high tide line and David piled it together carefully to make a fire. Max leaned back against a log and watched while Lucy opened a package of wieners and spread out the cloth on the sand.

David took charge of cooking wieners for everyone, and outdid himself by consuming an incredible number of hot dogs.

'You'll be sick when we start sailing,' Lucy warned him.

'I feel fine,' he told her. 'I won't get sick.'

The sheltered bay had just enough wind to allow them to sail away without starting the diesel engine. They drifted slowly out of the bay, gaining speed as they moved into the strong northerly wind.

Max moved to the mainsail line to adjust the sail, then looked over at Lucy. 'Should we take it on the port beam? Or turn and run with it?'

If they turned and took the wind on their port side they would have a fast, exciting ride towards Prince Rupert. If they ran, or turned until the wind was behind them, they would have a calmer, easier ride south towards Hunt's Inlet.

Lucy was at the wheel and he was giving her the choice. She could go back tonight, or stay for another day. Staying with Max was dangerous, and she was the girl who had spent years running away from that kind of danger. But when she went back, she was going to have to start working on saying goodbye to Max again. If she could put it off, let this day stretch another twenty-four hours——

She spun the wheel to starboard so that they took the wind behind them. She would not meet Max's eyes to see the look of triumph in them.

'This'll be an easier ride. David's going to get sick if we ride hard right now.'

'I never get seasick,' the affronted youngster denied. His healthy colour made nonsense of her concern. 'I like Hunt's Inlet. We were there before we came into Prince Rupert. You can sail the dinghy right into the inlet where there's an old quanset hut—used to be a big logging operation. From there there's a gravel road Dad and I hiked up. It goes all the way up to the top of the mountain. We saw wolves up there.'

'Calling it a mountain is a bit of an exaggeration,' Max told him. 'It's a hill.'

'Whatever!' The details didn't worry the boy.

Lucy had to agree that the little settlement was picturesque. It was about seven in the evening when they tied up to the small wharf. With the northern summer sun, they had about three hours of daylight left, but to David's disappointment, Max ruled that they didn't have enough daylight to go down to the mouth of the bay and explore the old logging camp. Instead, they went exploring the shore near the wharf, where summer cottages straggled along the shoreline. At the top of the ramp, they found a tiny road going in both directions. It wasn't wide enough for a car.

'They have a tractor,' Max told her. 'The government leaves a tractor here and they plough the road in the winter.'

'Surely they don't have a man working over here for only seventeen houses?'

'No, the locals do the work of operating it and keeping the path clear. Let's go this way, it's more picturesque.'

It was. The residents on the north end of the road had a lovely view of the ocean. They had peace and a beautiful wild setting and the best ocean view around. The houses seemed deserted, but Max and Lucy peopled the buildings with imaginary owners, as they wandered around cottages that had been abandoned and fallen into ruin, searching for hints of the lives that had been lived there. Just before dark, when the tide was at its lowest, David collected a bucketful of butter clams from the beach.

It was dark when they returned to *Wanderlust*. Max sent David to bed and his son went with no protest. It had been a long day and the sea air had exhausted them all.

'I'll get some clean salt water to soak these clams in, if you'd like to make us a coffee,' Max told Lucy. 'Then we can sit on deck and watch night fall.'

It was the nicest time of day for cruising folk. When Lucy brought the coffee mugs up, the sun had set and the moon showed the black land in sharp relief against the sky.

'Can we go for a walk again?' she asked. 'The moon is very bright.'

'That would be nice. Let's take our coffee with us.'

They took their mugs and strolled back up the ramp to the shore. When they had finished their coffee, they set their mugs on a fence post to pick up when they came back.

It seemed so natural when Max took her hand. 'It's been a beautiful day,' she told him. The path was clear in the moonlight, and underfoot, the grass was soft and silent. 'I can't remember when I've had such a good day.' She felt so full, so complete. She could feel the calm and the peace around her. It had seeped into her heart and she knew that this moment with Max, in this beautiful place, was something she must treasure, must keep alive in her memories for ever.

They came to the end of the road and looked out over the water. The wind had fallen light and the sea was smoothing into a glistening mirror for the moon above.

'There'll be others,' Max promised her. They stood together on the edge of the ocean, the edge of the world. She felt the security of his hand enveloping hers, his strength beside her, with her.

In the past, her body had said yes to him against her will. Tonight it was her heart that reached out towards him.

She stood so still that she could feel his heart beating through the hand that held hers. They stood together at the end of a nearly perfect day, and Lucy could see how it could be. A future with Max.

They had complemented each other so perfectly through the hours of the day. For hours she had forgotten to be wary, had relaxed and let things happen. She knew why Max had come, why he had followed her across a continent—because their minds and their bodies fitted together so perfectly, because they could go through this day each the perfect completion of the other. When she let herself, she could feel the bond between them, growing with each hour, each moment they spent together. She believed in that moment that if Max were in pain, she would feel his pain across an entire world.

And while she felt the bond, she felt also the torment within herself that made their union impossible.

'You can't go on forever denying what's between us, Lucy.' He combed her curls back gently with his fingers. 'You can feel the bond between us. It won't go away.'

She turned to him. She had both his hands in hers and she could feel the pain welling up. The past and the present and the future. Of all, the future would be the most painful—the loneliness and the agony of what could have been and what could never be.

'I don't deny it, Max.' A cloud slipped over the moon, dimming the world so that she shivered with the sudden cold. 'But I can't accept it either. I can't——'

'Lucy, the past is over.' He gripped her hands in the dark, feeling the trembling that was encompassing her body. 'Whatever it is that holds you to this man you married, you've got to let it go. He's not here now, and he hasn't been truly in your heart for a long time. If you still loved him, you couldn't respond to me the way you do.

The past may be his, Lucy, but the future is ours—yours and mine.'

If only it could be true!

'I'm cold, Max.' They turned away from the sea, back along the path. Lucy let her hand lie in his.

'His name was Ted,' she said flatly.

A seabird made a loud squawking noise on the other side of the bay, then flew away with a push of broad, strong wings.

'How did you meet him?' asked Max.

'The Consulate sent me back to the States after the hurricane. Mom's parents were dead and my Aunt Winifred landed up with me. She didn't want me. There was enough money to keep me at boarding school, and I was encouraged to visit friends during the holidays.'

The moon slipped out from behind the cloud, playing a beam of light over a well-tended rock garden beside the path.

'My last year of school, I stayed with a classmate during the Christmas break. I had no other family. My father hadn't talked to his family since he left England, so I didn't even know if any of them were alive. There was no one in the world that I could turn to. I felt that I didn't belong anywhere, and I wanted so badly to belong.'

There had been a party. She had dressed so carefully for it, hoping, dreaming that someone would be there, the white knight who would rescue her from lonely exile.

Where the path came to the wharf, they stopped walking, and Max pulled her back against him, holding her so that she leaned against his broad chest.

'When I met Ted at Dianne's house that Christmas, I was sure my dreams had all come true. I was swept off my feet, gloriously happy. Suddenly I wasn't a lonely kid any more; I was a girl who had a man, my own man. We planned our wedding for the week after my graduation that spring. I would go to Dianne's and be married from there.'

Lucy's hand clenched under Max's. She didn't want to be telling him this. More than anything, she wanted it behind her, buried and forgotten. She shivered in a sudden gentle breeze of cool air. Max moved away from her and she was alone again. Solitude was no stranger to her, but when Max was gone she felt the darkness growing around her. When he came back, he had a thick fisherman's sweater that he pulled over her head. She obediently pushed her arms into the armholes and let him pull the sweater down over her icy body. He sat down on a bench and pulled her against him, and after a moment she could feel his warmth.

'I was eighteen when we got married. Some eighteen-year-olds are pretty worldly, but I wasn't. My father had protected me, perhaps too much.'

'You were a virgin.' Max said it for her quietly.

'Yes, I was. Ted seemed to respect that. He kissed me and it was pleasant enough. If I thought of it at all, I suppose I thought the rest of it would be like those pleasant, undemanding kisses we shared.'

One night, in the garden of his parents' house, he had held her gently, almost reverently, and asked her to marry him. The garden, the moonlight, and the handsome young man could hardly have made a more romantic combination to her eighteen-year-old heart.

'All I knew, all I cared was that I was never going to be alone again. "And they lived happily ever after," was going to be my future, mine and Ted's.'

His friends and family had celebrated the wedding so joyously; kissing the bride, showering her with presents, sending them off together with laughter. 'It went wrong from the beginning—the first night. First I was nervous, then frightened. After that night, I tried to avoid him. Ted got increasingly angry—he hadn't got much of a bargain. I kept apologising. I still wanted to live happily ever after, but I wanted my nights spent alone.'

Ted. The Ted of her sleepless nights appearing suddenly at her bed, looming threateningly over her—demanding.

'Ted started drinking too much. One night he started telling me that he had rights, that I was his whether I wanted it or not. I didn't know what to do. I wanted to be a good wife to him, but I couldn't. When I started crying, it seemed to inflame him. He hit me, then took what he said was his.'

There had been no one to turn to, no one to run to. She could not face taking her bruises to a doctor, a stranger. When morning came, it seemed incredible, impossible—except for the painful bruising on her body.

'The next day, I believed him when he said it would never happen that way again.'

Max's arms were tight around her, as if he

could protect her from the past. 'It happened again?' He wanted her to say it hadn't, but he knew.

'I'd been in love with him—thought I was in love with him. The worst was when he drank. I kept hoping the drinking would stop. Sometimes he almost convinced me that it was my fault, that he had to hit me because I nagged him about his drinking, that I drove him to drinking because I didn't welcome him in my bed. I didn't think of leaving him—I don't know why, except that to me the rest of the world was frightening. I was so afraid of being alone, even my life with Ted seemed better than being alone.

'Then, one night, Ted didn't come home. I didn't call the police; I sat up waiting. In my mind I felt certain that he'd had an accident. I didn't call the hospitals, but I kept having this fantasy of the police coming and telling me he was dead in a traffic accident.'

Such a long, dark night. When he finally came home, he would be drunk. If she was sleeping, he would come into her room as she slept and she would waken to his threatening form over her. Better to be awake, prepared for what was coming.

'It was almost dawn when he came home, and by then I was really beginning to believe he might have been killed. When he walked in—I was disappointed.'

He had walked about their apartment, eating, shaving, washing. He'd talked to her. Through it all Lucy had sat, frozen, seeing him through a haze as a character in a play. He had explained nothing and she had asked nothing. She saw herself clearly as separate from him, and had a vision of her life without him. She saw herself at his funeral and there was no despair in her heart.

'I was disappointed when he came home. I know that's a terrible thing to say; I knew then that it was terrible. If I could want him dead, then staying with him was doing something destructive to me as a person.' She had been frozen for an hour after Ted had left, staring at nothing. She was still frozen when she stood up and started moving, packing.

'When he came home from work that night—if he came home—I was gone. That was eight years ago.'

Max cupped her face gently between his hands and she could see the sheen of moisture in his eyes. Only then did Lucy realise that her own face was wet with tears. He wiped her tears away gently.

'A year ago, in Toronto, who were you running from?' His voice was quiet, husky in the dark. 'Were you running from me, Lucy? Or were you running from Ted?'

When the door had closed behind Max that night, she had moved mechanically, without thought. From the moment when Max's form above her had turned into a nightmare memory of Ted, she had been reacting to past horrors. Not thinking, just running, knowing she must escape, must get away.

'I was running from Ted,' she admitted now, her voice faint on the night air. 'You see why it can't work with us, Max?' She touched his hand. 'You see why you've got to stop wanting me?'

'Shush!' he ordered her gently. 'You've shut all

this in and hoped it would disappear. You've got to let the tears out, you know. The hurt will be with you for ever until you let them out.'

Lucy shook her head. Crying tears from the heart was a weakness she couldn't afford.

'I was about David's age when my father died.' Max rubbed gently at the path where the silent tears had found their way down. 'We were very close, I loved him very much. I watched him die, but I wouldn't let myself break down. I was frozen and I felt nothing. I went to the funeral with dry eyes. Once I heard an aunt telling my mother how brave I was not to cry; but whenever the conversation turned to death or funerals, my hands would start to shake, my throat would go dry when I tried to talk.

'Mother and I were going through some papers about a year later, throwing out old papers and pictures of people neither of us could identify. Among the other pictures was one of my father and me working over an old bicycle of mine. With that picture in my hands I could feel all the pain, the loss that I'd denied ever since my father's death. I cried for him then, and it was only then that my hurt started to heal.'

She couldn't cry for herself, but she cried for the young Max's loss.

'You've had a bereavement, too, Lucy,' Max told her. 'You have to let yourself heal. You lost your parents, then you lost your husband. The man you fell in love with didn't exist. He was your hope for security and your dream of love wrapped into a man's body, so the disillusionment you suffered was as great a bereavement as any loss from death.'

'I don't want to cry!' she sobbed at him.

He pulled her gently to her feet and led her to *Wanderlust*.

'We've left our cups!' she protested.

'Tomorrow—they'll still be there.' Max slid open the hatch behind the cockpit and motioned her down the stairs. He lit a lantern and turned it low, then slid the hatch closed behind him and pushed her gently down.

Lucy sat and watched him. She was in his bedroom and she should be upset about that, but she didn't feel anything at all.

'This is your cabin,' she told him.

'Yes,' he agreed. 'I don't want you to be alone. Not tonight.'

'Max!' There was desperation in her voice. 'Max, you're supposed to go away now. You're supposed to understand that it's not going to work.'

He started to peel her sweater off. 'My mother always told me I was thick-headed.'

She had to laugh. 'Dammit, Max, she was right! What does it take to make you give up?'

'I don't give up.' He opened a drawer and found a pair of pyjama tops. 'Think you can wear these? I'll check on David while you change.'

When he came back, he had changed into the bottoms that matched the tops he had handed her. She had obeyed him, mechanically peeling off her clothes, buttoning his pyjama jacket. She watched him turn back the covers.

'In you get,' he told her.

'Max, I can't do it again. I don't want a marriage or an affair or anything.'

'You're too tired to worry about that tonight.

Get into bed. You need your sleep.' He pushed her down and lifted the covers over her. 'No passion tonight, I promise.'

It was crazy, but she believed him.

When he was in the bed beside her, he turned and held out his arms to her, and it seemed the most natural thing in the world to come into his arms and let him enfold her.

The emotional trauma had exhausted her, and she turned her head to rest her cheek on his arm. She was secure in Max's arms, and her breathing quickly slowed. His arm tightened around her in a sudden spasm, and she sleepily turned her body to rest more closely against his.

'Lucy?'

'Hmm?' She fought against returning to awareness. Her head rested comfortably on his arm. His other arm lay across her hip.

'Did you divorce him?'

'Who?' Her mind was miles away.

'Ted. Did you divorce him?'

'No. I never saw him or heard from him again.'

Her breathing deepened and she slept.

Max lay awake for a long time. In the darkest hour of the night the wind came up, buffeting *Wanderlust*. The motion disturbed the sleeping woman in his arms and she stirred against him. If she woke, he felt sure she would leave his bed. He lay very still, willing her to sleep on.

CHAPTER SEVEN

LUCY woke in Max's bed. Alone.

She lay quietly, listening to the sounds around her. Some time in the night the wind had fallen off. There was no sound of wind in the rigging, no waves lapping on the hull. The only sound she heard was the occasional murmur of voices in the forward section of the yacht. The only motion she felt was a slight movement as the man and boy moved about the boat.

When light footsteps came closer, she knew it was David and not his father.

'Are you awake, Lucy? I've brought you a cup of coffee.'

'I'm awake. Thanks! Just what I wanted.' She sipped at the hot coffee and let David tell her that the wind had fallen light, that they would probably be motoring to Prince Rupert today. David seemed unsurprised to find her in his father's bed. Was it because it was not an unusual event, or because with childlike innocence he attached no significance to her presence there?

'Dad listened to the marine forecast on the radio, and they predicted fog today,' he told her. 'That means I have to stand on the bow and spot for logs when we're underway.'

When David had left her, Lucy dressed and made Max's bed. She folded his pyjamas and put them away. Across from the bed there was a vanity mirror on a small raised dresser. She found brush and comb in the top drawer and brushed her hair vigorously.

Max was in the galley, generating delicious smells at the kerosene stove.

'How many eggs?' he asked her. 'Did you have a good sleep?'

She had lain in his arms all night, yet she felt no embarrassment in his presence. 'A lovely sleep. One egg, please. Can I help?'

'No. I'll let you clean up after we eat. I'll get us underway as soon as we've eaten. There's fog today, so we'll be going slowly, steering a compass course.'

He held out a piece of bacon for her and she bent her head to eat it from his fingers. 'Hmmm . . . that's good!'

'That's all you get until it's on the table.' She thought he was going to kiss her. His eyes were on her lips, then he turned away from her.

'Do you know how to make clam chowder?' he asked.

If he had kissed her, she would have kissed him back.

'Clam chowder is one of my best dishes,' she assured him. 'Do you want me to make it?'

Max nodded, watching the eggs. 'When we're underway. How do you want your eggs—over easy?'

'Yes, please.' If she responded to his kiss, fire would flare between them. Fire, passion, sex Nothing of that nature could flare up in her without Ted's ghost reappearing; she had to remember that.

She ate her eggs quickly, starting to clear the table before Max and David had finished. Max finished and added his plate to the pile of dishes she had stacked by the sink

'Come up when you're done,' he told David. 'I'll want you up front to spot for logs. Bring the handy talkie with you, and don't forget to put on your rain gear. It's not raining, but the air is wet from the fog.'

When David followed his father up, Lucy was left alone. She washed the dishes and put them away, then lit the kerosene cookstove to steam the clams. She searched for onions and celery and began chopping them for the chowder. When the engine started, she looked around to see if everything was stowed safely. It was supposed to be a calm day, but she took the precaution of making certain that nothing was in a position to go flying if the weather forecast was wrong.

She took her time over the chowder. It was going to be the best clam chowder Max had ever tasted, but he would probably never know that Lucy had shed tears into it while she cooked it for him.

It might take four or five hours to get back to Prince Rupert, but in her heart the weekend was over. She could see herself staying on *Wanderlust*, living and working wherever she and Max wanted to live and work. She could see herself being a mother to David—a good mother.

She could see it all, as clearly as she could see the chopped onions in her hands. But it wasn't real.

She was beginning to realise how much Max loved her. He was teaching her his love with his actions, not his words. If she let herself, she could give him back a love every bit as strong—every bit as deep as his own.

But when he touched her, between their passion and its fulfilment would be the memory of Ted. When he touched her and she shuddered, he would know that she could not see him, that the image of Ted was too large and too dark to allow her to see Max.

She couldn't bring Max happiness, only bitterness.

It was a slow run across Chatham Sound. They were in the middle of the Sound when Lucy dished out the chowder. She brought it up on deck in mugs so they could eat it with warm, fresh baked biscuits.

'You weren't exaggerating about your chowder.' Max had three helpings to prove his enthusiasm was real, and Lucy lost track of David's trips back to the soup pot.

Not a breath of wind stirred to encourage them to put up the sails. The fog lifted as they came into the harbour, but the wind eluded them still. They motored down the south side of the harbour and Max turned the vessel into his berth. Lucy helped David see that the dock lines were ready, then she stepped off with the forward line as Max brought *Wanderlust* alongside the wharf.

Max stepped off with the aft line. She left him and David to finish tying the yacht while she collected their mugs from lunch and took them below to wash. She heard Max making a radio-telephone call from the cockpit, but she couldn't make out his words over the engine sound. When the engine was shut down, he came below. He stood silently, watching her.

'Where's David?' She was suddenly and unaccountably nervous.

'He's gone to find his friends on the dock, to let them know he's back.'

Lucy dried the last dish and wiped the counter. She hung the damp dishcloth over the rail of the oil stove and put the drainboard away in its place. Max was standing too close to her, his hair damp and curling from the sea air.

'I don't know what you want me to do with the chowder,' she said. 'There's enough left to give you supper tonight.'

She was finished and she had to leave now, because staying would be insane. She went into the guest cabin. Her bag was there, but she had never used the cabin.

'I'll look after the chowder.' Max was standing in the passageway. He wasn't blocking her exit, so why should she feel he would not let her past?

'I have to go. It's time for me to go home.' It had been years since she had had a home to go to.

'Lucy?' Max stopped her with a hand on her arm.

He was only inches away from her, and she backed away, only to find herself up against the wall of the corridor.

He reached up and combed his fingers gently through her hair. She felt his touch clear down to her toes. 'It's getting to be a habit, your touching my hair.'

'I like the feel of your hair.' Max didn't take his hand away. He bent over to trail his lips along her throat. He was leaning against the wall, an arm on either side of her, and there was no way she could get away from his lips as they traced an erotic pattern down to the collar of her blouse.

He gently touched his tongue to the hollow of her throat. 'Lucy, I——'

She had to close her eyes against the look in his. 'Max, please!' She didn't know if she was asking him to stop or not.

He let his arms drop from the wall so that they could encircle her waist, and pressed his fingers against her waist. Lucy could feel his hands as if he traced patterns on her bare skin. His hands were still, but her skin felt his caress.

'I remember how it was that night in Toronto,' he told her. 'You needed me as much as I needed you.'

'Only at first,' she reminded him. He must also remember how, later, she had lain beneath him, her body cold to his touch.

He moved his hands up, but the movement stopped just below her breasts. His hand held her so gently, the slightest move would free her.

'I love the feel of you,' he whispered as his hands moved so slightly on her. Her eyes closed because there was no way she could deny that she, too, loved the feel of him.

'You should take advantage of this,' he whispered. 'You're safe right now. David is out there somewhere, talking to his friends, but, in a few moments he'll step on the boat and I'll have no choice but to stop making love to you.' He had moved his hands up to cup her breasts lightly.

Lucy shook her head, protesting this insanity, and grasped his wrists to pull them away from her breasts.

'Are you sure, Lucy?' His hands stilled their exploration. 'Whatever you feel about what comes after this, you can't deny that you like this part.' He trailed his finger from the hollow of her neck, down the vee of her blouse. Her hands dropped. David was outside; any moment he would come. She knew that was true.

Max's eyes were steady on hers and she could see the flecks of gold in the brown. His lips were open slightly, waiting, and she moved imperceptibly towards him.

He bent his head to her and his lips traced the path where his finger had been. 'Do you want me to stop?'

She shook her head mutely.

'You're safe, Lucy.' He opened the second button on her blouse, his hands strangely awkward on the thin fabric. 'Nothing can happen.'

Nothing? How could the delicious agony of his hands on her be described as nothing? His hands freed the last button and he pushed her blouse back. He kissed the tops of her breasts where they escaped from her bra, tormenting the aroused nipples through the thin lace.

'I have to go home,' she insisted weakly. 'This is no use, Max . . . not fair . . . not fair to you.'

He moved his hands to her back and drew her towards him. Her arms slid around his neck and their lips touched. If a speedboat roared by, or the wind howled above them, she would have heard nothing. The world swirled dizzily and she clung to him, opening her lips to him and tangling her hands in his hair as the depth of their kiss twisted their two souls together. When he raised his head, his breathing was husky, unsteady. Lucy had no breath at all.

He shook his head, holding her against him so

that the tops of her full breasts crushed against the rough cotton of his shirt. In the stillness, he watched her intently, then he drew her towards the open door of the guest cabin. He pulled her gently into the room and closed the door after her.

When she resisted, he stopped. They stood, his hand touching her wrist without exerting any pressure. Her heart beat wildly in her breast; her breath came raggedly. Outside, they heard laughter; David's voice on the wharf.

He would be back soon; Max was right. When David set foot on the boat, Max would release her. He would touch her and caress her, but that was all that could happen when David was awake and close by.

She met his eyes and knew that the decision was hers. Despite his hand on her wrist, Max would not force her to accept his caresses. She moved to him.

'You're crazy,' she whispered, standing before him.

'You're beautiful,' he whispered back, gently touching the side of a breast exposed by her open blouse. 'You don't know how beautiful.'

She came into his arms and he drew her down on to the settee. He bent his head to her, and she lifted her arms and gave herself up to him. She thought she would go mad with the beauty of the feelings that surged inside her. With his hands beneath the back of her thin blouse, Max ran his hands across her shoulders, down the curve of her spine, and she shuddered as he found places on her back that she had never known were sensitive to a man.

His hands wandered down, tracing the curve of her waist, stroking down over her hips through the denim fabric of her jeans. She reached up and pulled his head down tight against her, grasping his hair with a desperation that was foreign to her.

Her body arched against his, twisting in the ancient rhythm of love that she denied, wanting his touch on every part of her.

He pulled her hips against him, so that the strength of his passion was hard against her, and she gasped and held him tighter.

'Oh, Lucy!' he groaned. He caressed her hips, holding her hard against him, then his hands moved between them to find the fastener of her jeans. Lucy tensed as he slid open the zipper, but his hands moved away, caressing her sides and leaving her writhing as he traced a pattern around her breasts, always close but never touching the throbbing mounds.

He finally moved his hands to her breasts, teasing, caressing, then he bent over her and traced slowly with his lips from the underside of her jaw, to the hollow of her throat, then slowly all the way down to the white skin just above her waist.

She was aching, throbbing with the heat he had created inside her. She moved against him. She had no protest remaining. She knew she was not capable of stopping him from touching her in any way he wanted—that she wanted him to touch her with all the ways of love.

He pushed her away gently, bending to lay a featherlight kiss on her swollen lips. He fumbled with her blouse, fastening the buttons.

'David?' she asked. She had heard nothing.

'No, David isn't back.' He bent his head over the buttons. 'It's time to stop,' he smiled wryly, 'while I can.'

She watched the top of his head wordlessly as he fumbled with her buttons.

'Will you stay for dinner? Then I'll take you home.'

'Max——' He waited for her words, and she didn't even know what she wanted to say. 'Max, this is crazy—dangerous. We'll only hurt ourselves, playing with something that can't ever be.'

Max shook his head. 'I don't believe that.' He had finished the last button. He touched her face with a whisper of his fingers. 'For us it can be wonderful—It will be.'

'Max, I can't——'

'You will. Don't rush it—let tomorrow look after itself. Stay to dinner.'

Insane though it was, she stayed. David came in and they sat around the dinette table playing backgammon. Max, with his eyes on the swellings beneath Lucy's thin blouse, played terribly, and Lucy, her nipples hardening visibly in response to Max's thoughts, played hardly any better. David emerged as champion backgammon player, much to his delight.

'Let's play again,' he suggested exuberantly.

'No,' vetoed Max. 'Let's teach Lucy to play Lost Treasure.'

'Super! I'll get it. It's a great game, Lucy! You'll like it!' David dived into a hatch under the salon seat in search of this game.

Max reached across Lucy to collect the

backgammon pieces, and the back of his wrist brushed slowly against her breast.

Lucy jumped. 'Max!'

He grinned at her and she had to laugh, then gasped as he reached for the dice and his thumb brushed against her.

They played Lost Treasure, chasing elusive gold and silver treasures across a painted cardboard sea, following hints given by an electronic box. Lucy concentrated hard on the game, fighting a mental battle against the distraction of Max beside her. He sat with his arm casually over her shoulder, his thumb caressing the bare skin of her upper arm.

'I pirate you!' Lucy announced, moving her player beside Max's on the board.

'Go ahead,' he invited, and she laughed selfconsciously at the invitation in his low voice. They threw the dice and she won his plastic chests of gold and silver.

'You're playing terribly,' she told him.

'I know.' He ran his palm down the length of her bare arm as he leaned forward to pass the dice on to David. 'Your turn, son.'

'I think I'm going to beat you both!' the boy announced as he swooped his man down on Lucy's and pirated her treasure away.

'That's it! I've got a million now!' David informed them.

They agreed that David was the grand champion. Then Lucy got up to start dinner and Max moved to help her.

'No, I can do it alone,' she protested.

'I have to help,' he told her.

'That's right,' David agreed. 'It's Dad's day to

cook. You shouldn't be cooking for him at all. If you're going to cook, you have to let him help.'

Max reached for the mixing bowl she needed, setting it down slowly in front of her, and she gasped at his hidden touch.

'Did you hurt yourself, Lucy?' asked David with concern.

'It's all right,' she mumbled. She turned and pushed Max, hard. 'If I'm going to cook, you're staying out of the kitchen. Now, sit down!'

He laughed and let her push him away.

She shouldn't be letting this happen. Max and David, they were getting far under her skin and the parting was going to hurt like nothing in this world. She should be walking away.

They ate and David started the dishes, but Lucy insisted on helping him by drying. They walked on the wharves after everything was cleaned up. Max and David discussed the boats they passed, and Lucy was content to listen to them. Max took her hand in his and their coupled hands swung gently as they walked.

David found a friend and became involved in trying to fix the chain on the other youngster's bicycle, while Max walked on with Lucy until they came to the end of the dock. They sat on the rail at the side of the wharf, watching the sunset on the other side of the harbour.

'I'm flying to Toronto tomorrow,' he told her abruptly. 'I have some urgent business to look after.'

'Oh.' He hadn't said what it was. The sun was low on the horizon, setting, and some of the light had gone from the day.

'Would you stay here and look after David

while I'm gone? There was one cancellation on the flight from Vancouver to Toronto. I couldn't get two seats.'

That explained the radio-telephone call. He had called to reserve his flight to Vancouver, then from Vancouver to Toronto. Why?

'Will you stay with him, Lucy?' he asked again. 'There's no one else I can ask.'

'Yes, of course I will.' She got to her feet because she couldn't sit still any more. 'If you're going tomorrow you'd better show me where things are—the engine water intake valve, the bilge pump control. How long will you be gone?'

'I don't know. At least three days. I have to——' he broke off and shook his head. 'I'll phone you at work to let you know.'

'I'd better go home now.' Lucy moved abruptly. 'Show me what I need to see on *Wanderlust* and I'll go. I need to get some sleep before work tomorrow morning.' He had said earlier that he would take her home, but that was unnecessary, and she told him so. 'My car is here. I'll just drive home.'

'I'll walk you to the car,' he told her quietly when they had finished going over the essential valves and switches on *Wanderlust*, and Lucy didn't argue because she would get away quicker if she agreed with him. Max seldom lost arguments anyway, and she had a terrible need to get away from him.

In the parking lot, she dug her keys out of her bag, but Max leaned on the driver's door, effectively stopping her from getting into the car.

'Lucy, can I ask you something?'

'You've never hesitated before.' He had asked

her all manner of things, things she had never shared with anyone before.

He nodded, acknowledging the truth of that. 'Why didn't you divorce Ted? You could have divorced him years ago. Why did you stay married? Why did you keep his name? In spite of—Well, do you still love him?'

'No! How could I?' She shook her head vehemently. 'I hoped he would die so I could escape. How could I love him when I felt like that? I thought about getting a divorce—but if I filed a divorce suit against him, I couldn't help feeling that he might find me. If I went away and just disappeared, he would never find me.' But Max had found her. Max had followed and found her.

Lucy turned her car keys in her hand. It was time for her to go, more than time to go.

'And the name?' Max insisted. 'You could have gone back to using your own name—I would have thought you would want to, if you hated him so much.'

'I didn't want to. As long as I kept that name, I couldn't forget. As long as I remembered, I would never let myself get into that position again—never let a man talk me into marriage again.'

He reached across and imprisoned her hands. He drew her towards him, pulling her hands until she was trembling against him. He bent his head to her then and brushed her lips softly with his. When he freed her hands, Lucy made no move to escape him; she couldn't. He bent his head again and took her lips with a hard passion that left her clinging to him for support. His hands moved down the curve of her back, shaped her hips to him so that she had no doubt of his need of her. His kiss invaded the depths of her until she was dizzily drowning in his embrace.

She pushed away from him when he raised his head. She was terrified at the emotions raging in her, at the storm he was able to rouse in her body. She fumbled with the keys in her hand, and Max reached a hand to caress her neck.

'Max!' she protested.

'That's one promise you're not going to keep,' he told her. 'I'll see to that.'

CHAPTER EIGHT

HER apartment was cold and empty. She wasn't hungry, but she opened her refrigerator and stared at the empty shelves, seeing Max walking away from her in the parking lot. He'd turned her to a quivering mass of jelly, then walked away with that crack about her promise.

He'd better be wrong. Marriage to Ted had been a disaster, but when she left him she had been able to put her life back together. But Max—

She had thought that her cool response to Ted's lovemaking indicated a lack of passion, but Max was teaching her differently. The passion he aroused in her was terrifying. Even more terrifying was her growing emotional need of him. Afterwards, would there ever be a spark to her life again?

When she left Ted she had sworn that she would never again let any man be her lover. She looked down at her shaking hands. If Max came knocking on her door tonight, would she let him in? If he touched her, would she push him away?

In Toronto, in her apartment with his hands caressing her body to flames, she had suddenly frozen in fear. He had left when she told him to go. If he had stayed, would she have been able to push him away? Had she ever been able to push him away?

She was filled with the sudden certainty that if he came, she would be powerless against him. He must know this about her; she had no secrets from him. He pierced her eyes with his own and she had no part of herself that was private from Max.

Terrified, she grabbed up her handbag and flung out of the apartment. The man next door ducked out of her way, muttering that she was a strange one.

Lucy left her car at the kerb; she couldn't trust herself to drive in this state of mind. She slung her bag over her shoulder and started walking, oblivious of the rain that had been threatening ever since the sun set.

She crossed the small city in the rain. No one noticed her. It was Sunday evening and the residents were indoors, not watching for the woman walking, head bent against the windblown rain. When she came to a familiar house, she realised she was tired and cold and miserable. She was so tired of sitting alone with her dreams and nightmares. Opening up her past with Max had left her more vulnerable, and tonight she was frightened of her own company.

Janice flung open the door to her.

'Lucy! Come on in. My goodness, you're soaked! Where have you been? John's been frantic, calling constantly.' She pushed Lucy over to the fire. 'Take off your jacket.'

Lucy let Janice peel her out of her jacket.

'That won't do!' Janice surveyed her disapprovingly. 'Your jeans are soaked. Go into the washroom and strip down. I'll get you a robe to put on and a hot drink. Come on, now—move,

Lucy! You'll be frozen soon. You can't stay wet like that on a night like this.'

'What about Jim?' Lucy looked around in faint dismay.

'He's gone—to the Charlottes.'

'What?' asked Lucy stupidly. Jim gone?

'He had a contract to fly the plane over to the Queen Charlotte Islands for a logging operation there. He'll be back in two days—they have some surveying to do over there and they need the plane until Tuesday.'

Janice pushed Lucy into the bathroom.

Lucy undressed slowly and towelled herself dry. She felt oddly detached from the events around her. She rubbed her legs hard with the towel and concentrated on Janice and her family. Amanda would be in bed. If Jim was away on a flight for a logging company on the Queen Charlotte Islands, that must mean Jim's one-man chartering business was going well. Last year Janice and Jim had put up everything they owned to buy a floatplane for Jim to charter commercially.

Janice led the dried, tousled Lucy into the sitting room.

'Drink your coffee,' she instructed. 'Drink it up and I'll get you another one. You need the stimulus.'

'I'm all right,' protested Lucy.

'You don't look all right. You look awful!'

'Thanks,' she laughed weakly, 'I needed that. I take it Jim's absence means business is doing well.'

'Yes, but——' Janice broke off. 'Don't you think you should call John?'

'No. Why?'

'He's frantic about you. He's been trying to get hold of you ever since Saturday morning. He called you every half hour on Saturday. He kept calling me, too. He doesn't know where you are and he's worried.'

Lucy shook her head. 'I don't belong to him. He has no right——' She wondered if John was being possessive, or if she had given her friends just cause for concern by leaving without saying anything. 'Were you worried?'

Janice grinned. 'Well, I had inside information. Cheryl has been talking of nothing but the sexy Max McGraw.'

Was the mere mention of his name enough to make her heart thunder?

'I do remember that name, you know,' said Janice. 'Last year when we put Drake Brothers on computer we had a lot of trouble with the payroll. You and I made a list of the questions we had, then you had me call S.C.S. in Toronto and ask you how to deal with it. I remember it very well, because part of your instructions were not to mention your name under any circumstances. I asked for the chief programmer, and they gave me Mr McGraw.'

'He's the owner,' Lucy explained. 'He is the chief programmer, but he doesn't call himself that.'

Janice took Lucy's empty cup and refilled it. 'Drink that! I'm heating up some leftover roast for you, too.'

'I'm not hungry.' Lucy accepted the coffee and sipped it. She was warmer now, but the feeling of unreality persisted. 'I had supper—clam chowder.'

'Did you spend the weekend with him?'

Lucy nodded. 'We went sailing.' Janice's eyes widened and Lucy added quickly, 'His son was there, too. We just sailed—that's all.' That was so far from the truth that her voice lost its conviction.

'Are you going to phone John? I know I'm being nosey, Lucy, but I care about you. You're my friend and I want you to be happy.'

'It's all right.' Somehow Janice's questions did not threaten her tonight. 'No, I'm not going to phone John. I have nothing to say to him.'

'But you and Max—that's not working?' Obviously it wasn't working or Lucy would not have appeared tonight at her door, silent and bedraggled.

Lucy shook her head. 'I don't think I can talk about it, Janice.'

They sat in front of the fire in silence until Lucy spoke at last.

'Max is going to Toronto tomorrow. David—his son—is staying behind, and I'll be staying on the boat to look after him.'

'How did Max and the boat get to be here?' queried Janice, 'This is a long way from Toronto. And what sort of boat is it?'

'A forty-six-foot sailboat. They bought it in Vancouver and sailed it up here.'

Janice whistled. 'A yacht, then, not a mere boat. You could live in something like that, travel around the world. Is it anything like the yacht your family used to have?'

One night, when they were both exhausted from working overtime to meet a deadline for one of their clients, they had exchanged childhood experiences. Lucy hadn't talked about those happy childhood years to many people, but Janice had been easy to talk to.

'The same size,' she told Janice. 'There are a lot of similarities.' The movement of the boat on the water . . . the feeling of sailing . . . the freedom . . . the wild sense of exhilaration . . .

'He's a long way from home,' mused Janice. 'Three thousand miles from Toronto. Why didn't he buy a boat on the east coast? Why is he here? He can have a ball exploring the east coast of Canada, down to Florida and the Caribbean. What is he doing out here?'

'Looking for me,' admitted Lucy. 'He came looking for me.'

Janice was speechless. 'Then why are you looking so miserable? If he's anything like as fantastic as Cheryl says——'

'He is.'

'Then what's wrong?'

Lucy pushed restlessly to her feet. 'I hear Mandy. Can I get her?'

Janice shook her head. 'She's just talking in her sleep, she'll be quiet in a moment. The roast should be hot—I'll get it.'

Lucy followed her to the kitchen and helped slice bread and set the table for the two of them. When the roast was in front of her, she found she was hungry after all. She took a piece of fresh bread and heaped beef and gravy over it.

'This is good,' she told Janice. 'You're a fantastic cook.'

'I'm glad you came to eat it. I never eat properly when Jim is away. I made the roast, but I couldn't eat it at supper. Eating alone is depressing, and Mandy doesn't eat much meat.' Janice was doing justice to the roast now, eating as she talked.

'I was married before, you know,' Lucy told her. 'I guess I'm still married to him.'

Janice watched her intently. 'Not good?'

'I left him—eight years ago.'

Lucy managed to finish her plate, but she had lost her appetite. She stacked the few dishes from their meal and moved to the sink.

'You don't mind if I start washing them, do you?' she asked. Some people were touchy about their kitchens, but Janice wasn't one of them. She got out the washing up liquid for Lucy and found a tea-towel. She didn't tell Lucy that the dishes could more easily be stacked in the dishwasher; she thought Lucy needed the therapy of work.

'Why did you leave him?' she asked. 'Did you love him?'

Lucy carefully wiped the plate in the soapy water. She gave it a rinse and put it on the draining board for Janice to dry. 'I don't know what I felt by the time I left him. I was—a battered wife.'

She had never used those words before, and somehow it removed her from what Ted had done to her. Battered wife. You heard about them on the news, in the movies, in books. There were so many others.

'You were right to leave,' Janice told her. 'It's not good to stay, not good for the husband or the wife. My sister——' she broke off, then shook her head. 'That's not my story to tell, but you're different. You wouldn't stand for that, wouldn't let a man do that to you.'

'I did. For two years I did.'

'Then you've changed. Of course you've changed in the years since you left him.' Janice put the last dish in the cupboard with a bit of a bang.

'Have I? I don't know.' Lucy turned on the tap and rinsed the sink. Crossing an ocean, she would have used salt water for rinsing up rather than waste precious fresh water. Would she ever cross an ocean again?

'What if he came back now? What if this husband of yours turned up tomorrow and wanted his so-called "rights"?'

Ted on her doorstep, demanding his rights? Somehow she couldn't believe in it. Max had pursued her across a continent, but had Ted really cared that much? She could hardly remember the shape of his face. In her memories he was a shadow, hazy and without form.

'It doesn't scare you, does it?' queried Janice.

'If it happened, it would. It just doesn't seem real. If it happened—I'd kick him out, that's all.'

Lucy realised with amazement that it was true. The Ted she had married had been a bully, but Lucy had grown strong and she was a survivor. She had grown strong, and she was convinced that although she had been a victim while they were married, today she could dominate him with her will. Yes, of course she had changed.

'Will you stay the night?' asked Janice, and Lucy accepted, feeling unwilling to go back out into the cold, wet night.

'Will I get to see the yacht you're babysitting?' asked Janice later.

'Yes, of course. Come to dinner tomorrow. If

Jim is still going to be away, you can bring Amanda down to the *Wanderlust* and have dinner with David and me.'

'I'd love too—so would Mandy. How old is this boy, David? How are you going to manage to look after him? For how long?'

'What do I answer first?' laughed Lucy. 'He's twelve, and he's pretty independent. I guess Max figures he'll be all right on his own during the day, but I thought I would just come in to the office mornings. Max will only be away for a few days. I can take work home—to the boat, I mean.'

'Don't,' suggested Janice. 'Let me pick up some of the load you're carrying at work. I've been training Cheryl to do quite a bit of my job, so I can manage the time.'

Should she take the time off, as if it was a holiday? Spending the time with David would be immensely satisfying; but playing the part of surrogate mother to Max's son would only entangle her further, make things harder in the end.

CHAPTER NINE

WHEN Janice and Lucy returned from Princess Fishery the next day, Max and David were waiting in the office. Max had taken David to a vacant cubicle and was coaching him on inputting a computer program.

When Lucy touched Max, he turned swiftly to her, and his smile and his hand on her arm took her breath away.

'I hope you don't mind us using it?' he gestured to the computer. 'Cheryl said it wouldn't be busy for another half hour.

'Of course I don't mind. Max, you haven't met Janice yet—but I've told you about her. Janice, this is Max McGraw, the driving force of S.C.S.'

'Lucy's right hand,' declared Max as he shook hands with Janice. 'I've heard about you. If you're ever in Toronto looking for a job, you'll let me know?'

Janice flushed with pleasure. 'I talked to you once at S.C.S.'

'From Prince Rupert,' Max remembered. 'You had a customer with a holiday pay problem. Did the changes I suggested work?'

'Yes, perfectly. The client was very pleased—Can I corrupt David with some games? We have a disk of games.'

'Why not? If nothing else, Pac-Man teaches good eye-hand co-ordination!'

Janice pulled up a chair beside David and

flipped through a tray of disks beside the computer.

'How about this, David! Galaxy Games, Adventure, Bulls and Bears——'

As Janice slipped the disk into the disk drive, Max touched Lucy's shoulder. The way his touch sent her heart pounding, it was a good thing he was going away. She must get control of her reactions!

He led her into her own office and closed the door behind them. She moved nervously to her desk and shuffled some papers.

'I've arranged to have my afternoons free,' she told him. 'I thought David could come in with me in the mornings. He seems to like spending time on the computer.'

'He loves it.' Max picked up a paperweight from her desk. 'I'll have to call you from Toronto to let you know when I'll be back.'

'Is everything all right at S.C.S.?' He hadn't said why he was leaving—hadn't explained what was so urgent that he should fly across the continent, leaving his son behind.

'Everything's under control. Chan can handle it—it's not as hard as it was—nor as exciting.' Max carefully set her paperweight back on her desk. 'The program is pretty well perfected—now it's a matter of keeping it up to date. I haven't been very involved in administration for some time now.'

She knew Max had always regarded the business end of S.C.S. as merely a necessary partner to the creative process. She knew, also, that Max could not be idle. If he hadn't already begun a new project, he would soon.

'I hope you have a good flight,' she said.

Something in her words made him say, 'Don't run away from me again, Lucy.'

She shifted another page on her desk. She had made a thorough mess of the papers relating to Dr Fletcher. 'I can't go anywhere—I'm looking after David.'

'I know.' He grinned. 'Why do you think I asked you?'

Airlines weren't booked to capacity these days, so David was staying behind to ensure that Lucy didn't run while Max wasn't looking. She should have known. Perhaps, deep down, she had known.

He reached a hand to touch her, but she turned away.

'Lucy, there are things that have to be settled—something I have to do. When I get back, we'll talk. Maybe you're not thinking of San Francisco or Tahiti, but you haven't stopped running from me. When I get back, it'll be time to settle this.'

Yes, but not the solution Max wanted.

She was ready for him to kiss her, so that she was shocked when he left quickly, without even touching her. It was only as he left that she felt how strongly she had desired some touch from him before he left.

But he was gone.

Dr Fletcher's affairs kept Lucy busy until noon. She took David to lunch then, knowing she couldn't get away as early as she had planned. They ate sandwiches at a delicatessen, talking about computers and sailboats.

'Have you liked living on a sailboat, David?' Lucy asked.

'Yeah! We've been to so many places. I was never out of Ontario before. Now I've flown across Canada. I've been to Alaska. I've been to hot springs, to deserted old indian villages with totem poles—so many places!'

'Do you miss your friends? Your school?'

David wolfed the second half of his sandwich and started on his milk. 'Sometimes. Mostly, I miss Grandma. She's pretty strict, but she's okay. I'd like to see the guys from my school in Toronto, but I've met a lot of people since we moved on to the boat, and I've got friends everywhere now, all over the coast. What I really miss is getting to the libraries. Grandma says I'm a bookworm, she says Dad shouldn't let me read so much; but Dad says reading never hurt anyone. I was reading about dinosaurs when we left Toronto. We've got lots of books on the boat, but not about prehistoric times. I don't think Dad is really very interested in dinosaurs.'

That solved the immediate problem of what to do about David. Lucy armed him with her library card, Do-It-Yourself's phone number, and dropped him at the library.

'Call me when you're done, David, and I'll pick you up.'

Back at the office, she started trying to plough through an immense amount of work. A visit from Statistics Canada tied up a further half hour of her time. She answered a series of seemingly senseless questions while the government statistician filled in a five-page form.

'You said you'd be back next month?' she asked when the form was finally complete.

'Next month,' he agreed dolefully, 'and the month after. You've been chosen as part of the sample for the six-month study.'

'Just my luck,' she muttered.

'The names are chosen randomly,' he explained. 'The computer selects a number of businesses randomly each time a new sample is needed. The chances are that you will never be selected for another survey after this.' His words came out with the lack of conviction of one who has recited the same explanation to many people, and never been believed.

'It's all right. You have to get your figures from somewhere, I know that. If you could let us know the day before you come back, we'll have the figures ready for you. Just call and tell Cheryl, our receptionist.'

'Thanks,' he made a note in his little book. 'It does help if you have the figures ready ahead of time. Thank you very much for your co-operation.'

He left just before David called.

'Everything okay?' Lucy asked Janice. 'Can you handle it if I leave now?'

'No problem.'

'Okay, I'll go now. Don't forget, you and Amanda are having dinner with me tonight.'

'I'm not likely to forget—I've never been on a sailboat before. Are you sure you want to bring Mandy? She might be a handful on a boat!'

She might have been, but David took to Amanda on sight. He sat on the floor with her, handing her shells and pots to play with, playing peek-a-boo with her when she tired of banging pots, and generally keeping her away from the contents of bookcases and cupboards. When supper was ready, it was David who perched Amanda in the corner of the seat at the table, piling pillows on both sides of the baby in an attempt to confine her.

'It's more like a high chair that way,' he told the two women. He carefully fed her from the bowl Lucy had dished out. Amanda solemnly watched him, obediently opening her mouth for each bite. Janice resisted telling David that Mandy had been feeding herself for months; that normally she wouldn't let anyone else feed her.

Mandy's eyes were drooping by the time dinner was over, so Lucy and Janice settled her in the forward cabin where the berth had no open sides for a toddler to fall out. David tried to insist that he do the dishes, but Lucy protested.

'We'll take turns, David. I'll do them tonight, and Janice can help me. Tomorrow you can have your turn washing up.'

He eyed her doubtfully, but hopefully. 'Dad said I should——'

'You've already helped with cooking dinner. You could take the garbage up for me. I think that's enough for tonight.'

'Okay, and—Could I stop at the *Julie II* and see Gerry?'

'That's your friend who lives on the blue fishing boat, isn't it? Sure you can see him. Be back by eight.'

When David had gone, Janice and Lucy worked on the dishes.

Janice was entranced by the interior of

Wanderlust. 'I can't get over this kitchen. A place for everything—and all that beautiful wood! What kind of wood?'

'Teak. Teak is good on boats,' Lucy explained. 'It has so much natural oil that it will never rot. You sand it and oil it and it looks like this—a nice warm wood finish.'

'I like it. I'd never have believed a boat could be so big and beautiful inside. You'd never imagine all this room from a look at the outside.'

'Sailboats are like that—Here, hand me that frying pan behind you, on the stove.' Janice reached the cast-iron pan and passed it, and Lucy slipped it into the soapy water. 'Sailboats are low in the water, so much of the boat is actually under water. It's deceptive from the outside.'

They finished the dishes and Janice wiped down the table while Lucy polished the metal plate behind the stove.

'It is nice. That kitchen amazes me—even a microwave oven!' Janice exclaimed.

'It only works if the generator is going; or if Max is plugged into shore power.'

Janice frowned, looking around herself. 'So beautiful, but I don't think I could live here. I'd miss having a yard.'

'The world for your back yard,' murmured Lucy with a smile. 'You'd be surprised how it feels—freedom—take your home with you and go where you want.'

'Is Max going to keep living on the boat? Or is it a holiday for him?'

'I don't know. I haven't been enquiring into Max's future plans.' It was a dangerous area of conversation for her and Max. 'He might wander, but he's got that tie with S.C.S., and I think he'd find things to work at wherever he was. I think, for him, the boat is a way of escaping, of giving himself some freedom.'

'And what about you?' asked Janice. 'Will you be with him?'

'No. Whatever Max McGraw does with his life, he won't be doing it with me.'

Someone else? She envisaged Max with a tall, lissom brunette at his side . . . sailing hard . . . spray and wind on their glowing faces. She had no right to mind. Max should have someone; he needed someone at his side.

When Janice was gone, and David back home and in bed, the quiet was haunted. Lucy lit the kerosene lanterns in the salon and turned them low to give a warm light. She could have turned on Max's colour television to watch the news, but she curled up beside Max's bookshelves instead.

They were there, as Max had told her: *The World is my Backyard* and *Around the World in Lucy Anne* by Barry Jamieson. She hadn't seen the brown bindings in years, but they were as familiar as yesterday afternoon. Freud might have a reason for her not having a copy of her father's books. Her father's copies had been aboard *Lucy Anne* when she went down in the storm-tossed Caribbean, and her aunt wouldn't have smiled on reminders of the irresponsible, restless life style her sister's family had led. There were bookstores and libraries with copies, and it had been years since Aunt Winifred's wishes had guided Lucy's actions; but she had never bought a copy, never looked for her father's name in a bookstore or a library.

Lucy picked up the first book her father had written, turning it in her hands, seeing the well-worn binding. She opened it and leafed through the pages, seeing that the book had been read and read again, the pages turned often. She read the words of the dedication, 'To my wife Anne, and to Lucy, the child we made together.' She turned the page.

'My father lived in a large house, on a large farm. Our back garden was big, green, and well-tended. As I grew up in that well-cultivated English garden, I began to feel the restless stirrings of all youth the world over.

'When I was seventeen, luck brought a sailing yacht into my life. *Orion* was a large schooner, and her owners needed a crew of six to sail her. While *Orion* was anchored near our village the youngest, most junior sailor was hospitalised with appendicitis. Hoping to turn the lad's misfortune into my opportunity to see the world, I borrowed a dinghy and rowed out to where *Orion* was anchored. I must have convinced the captain that I would work hard enough to make up for my lack of expereince, for he hired me. I worked hard, sometimes I slaved. And I learned that for my own backyard I wanted—the world.

'*Orion* left the coast of Britain on a rainy September day; her new, green sailor aboard . . .'

Her father's words caught her, as they had so many other readers. For her, the enchantment was double. This resourceful, gentle man had met and married her mother. Her memories of him were a child's memories, barely glimpsing the scope of the man in a man's world.

She was no longer a child. The love story of

Barry and Anne gripped her. She cried when they left the U.S.A., leaving Anne's unhappy family behind; when, in a lonely bay in Tahiti, Anne lost their first child. As a youngster, she had known of the loss, but not understood the tragedy of it. The birth of Lucy herself a year later was celebrated with joy, but the Jamiesons did not feel it called for them to give up their adventurous life. They celebrated Lucy's first birthday at a public wharf in Panama. The other boaters at the wharf threw a party, showering her with goodwill. A fisherman had given her a hand-carved rattle. An Australian yacht-owner's wife had given handmade denim coveralls . . .

It was late when Lucy put her father's book down. At the back of the book were pictures, and she examined them carefully . . . the *Lucy Anne* . . . herself as a child . . . far-off places she remembered, people she had met in those places . . . her mother and father together, looking at each other with no awareness that any other person existed.

Lucy doused the kerosene lamps, leaving one burning low in case David woke in the night. She looked into the forward cabin to see that David was sleeping and his light out. She had read the events of her young life, told from a viewpoint different from her own memories. Throughout the book, the tremendous bond between her parents shone through between her dead father's words. Their love for each other had been so deep a part of their lives that neither could have been complete without the other.

Her mother must have looked in on the sleeping young Lucy many nights, before going back to the cabin she shared with her husband—her lover. In the after-cabin of *Lucy Anne*, in all the places they had explored together, Barry and Anne must also have shared the joys of love with each other.

Lucy's overnight bag was where she had left it, in the side guest cabin. She changed into a light cotton nightgown. The settee had not been made up into a bed yet. She knew the bedding was stored in a hatch under the seat.

Max's bed was already made up. In the morning she would be up before David. She didn't think he would know—or care—where she had slept. Certainly Max would not mind her sleeping in his bed, she reflected as she curled up under the covers of the wide double bed in the cabin at the back of the boat. He had spent enough time trying to get her into his bed, he was hardly likely to object to her choice of a sleeping place.

She had left the books in the saloon. In the darkness, in Max's cabin, her parents seemed very close. To the young Lucy their joint tragedy had seemed the act of an unfair God, but now, she wondered what life would have been for either of them, alone. They had lived their short lives fully, loving more and seeing more than most people who lived to an old age. Given the choice, would either Barry or Anne have chosen to live slow, sedate lives on land as the price for a few more years? She didn't think so.

If Lucy was the woman her mother had been, she would strike out for love and adventure with Max McGraw.

'But I'm not,' she whispered in the darkness. Perhaps if Ted hadn't destroyed her ability to love, to trust her life and her future to anyone but herself—perhaps then she and Max . . .

Max was gone, but his presence wouldn't leave her. It must have been David, with his sandy hair and his slow smile; David trying to look after her in the quiet, unobtrusive way Max did. It was David who wouldn't let her forget Max's presence.

When she woke, she realised with surprise that she had slept well, without the dreams that haunted her sleep so often. She and David had a breakfast of bacon and eggs before going to the office. David happily glued himself to the computer until coffee time, then Lucy sent him to get some doughnuts for everybody.

When John called, she evaded his invitation to go out for dinner and dancing.

'I can't, John. Max has had to fly back to Toronto for a few days, and I'm staying with his son while he's gone.'

'His son?' Of course, John didn't know about David, about *Wanderlust*. 'Lucy, what are you getting into? This man—his son—come out of nowhere and suddenly you're up to your neck with them?'

'I've got to run, John. We've just had a computer run crash.' Why was she lying? Couldn't she handle this without lying?

'Lucy, when——'

'Call me at the beginning of next week.'

'I've tried to call you at home, tried every night. There's no answer. Lucy, I want to know just——'

'John, there's nothing to know. Call me at the office on Monday. I've got to go.' She hung up. Hanging up on John was getting to be a habit.

John had been good company until he had

tried to get too close, to break the barrier Lucy kept between herself and the rest of the world.

She thought about her father and mother and the love they had shared. They had been two people joined, facing the world as one. They had known each other deeply; loved not blindly, but with clear vision. John's vision of her was rose-tinted; he had never seen the real Lucy.

Nor had Ted. She and Ted had been strangers living together, acting out their insecurities against each other. Why had she let herself be Ted's victim? She had been only eighteen when she married him, but she had been an eighteen-year-old who had seen the world, who could look after herself alone. Ted had hurt her, but she had let him. She could have left any day; no one had made her stay those two years.

And having left, why keep his name? Ted couldn't hurt her now; she wouldn't let him hurt her again. There was no reason why she could not find him, ask for a divorce. Surely he would consent. It could be no joy to him to be legally tied to a wife who had deserted him years ago.

She was not Lucy Carter. She was Lucy Jamieson, son of Barry and Anne, not the wife of Ted Carter.

She would sit down and write to Ted, ask him for a divorce. Not today, but soon.

She took David for dinner at Smiles Restaurant that night, then they went to the movies together to watch a space age fantasy that Lucy enjoyed almost as much as David. Back at the boat, they each had a shower in Max's newly installed shower, then tumbled into bed.

Once more, Lucy slept in Max's bed.

David was scheduled for an all-day hike from the community centre on Wednesday, so Lucy dropped him off on her way to work. The next day David hoped to accompany his friend Gerry on the fishing boat *Julie II* for a four-day fishing trip. Lucy was stalling. She felt Max would not object, but she was unwilling to give her permission before talking to him.

As if he knew she wanted to talk to him, Max telephoned just after she arrived at the office that morning.

'How is everything, Lucy?' He sounded as if he was next door, not three thousand miles away in Toronto.

'David's fine, and the boat is fine.' She was breathless, as if she had been running. 'Where are you? It doesn't sound like S.C.S.—too noisy!'

'The airport . . . and is Lucy fine?'

Was she? 'Which airport?'

'Toronto International—what are you doing now?'

'Well, I've been drowning in Dr Fletcher's affairs. You remember, I was telling you he hired me to do a consultation for him?'

'I remember. As a matter of fact, on my stopover in Vancouver, I had a talk with an equipment distributer who seems willing to work with you. He'll be sending you a letter this week with price lists, equipment specifications, and your discount rates,' Max told her.

'Thanks, Max—that should solve part of my problem. The rest of it is starting to shape up. I worked on it most of yesterday and I've got a good start on flowcharting what I need for the medical billing. Today I'm going to finish roughing it out, then I'll try to assess what part of the programming I can do myself. I don't really know what I'll do about the rest of it.'

'You'll give it to me to do,' he told her easily. 'What else would you do?'

'Max——' this was getting ahead of her. 'Max, I don't know if that's a very good idea. I'm not ready for——'

'Then we'll make it a business deal. We'll draw up a contract.'

'If it's a business deal, then you know I can't afford you!' Max hadn't paid for that boat by charging dime store prices.

'You don't have to pay, Lucy. The medical program is something I can make money out of once we get it written—the market is Canadawide if we write modules to look after the quirks of each province's billing system. We split the S.C.S. profits on the sales between us—maybe your company should distribute in the West—we can work out the details.'

It would work, and she had no doubt that Max could make money on it for both of them while making a lot of doctors happy with their computer systems. It would be fun, working with Max again. Together, they could really make something of what she had started here in Prince Rupert. But there were personal considerations. If she let Max stay and help her, would she ever be free of him?

'Max, I have to think about it. I don't know—I know it would be good business, but——'

'Take your time,' he agreed. 'I'll give you until Sunday.'

'Sunday? Will you be back then?' Would she

have herself together, ready to face Max in person by Sunday?

'Yes. I'd be sooner, but I have to fly down to the States for a brief trip. Is everything all right there until Sunday?'

'I think so. What about the batteries? Should I run the engine to charge them again? It's the same engine we had on *Lucy Anne*.'

'All right,' he agreed. 'Run it for an hour, maybe an hour and a half, watch the ammeter and run it until the charge rate drops. Can you do that?'

'Of course. I've done it on *Lucy Anne* lots of times. What about water?'

'You won't have any problem with water. I filled up last week, so you've still got more than two hundred gallons. Is David helping you with the housework and cooking?'

'Yes, he's working hard. We've been eating out some, because I've been getting tied up at work. Max, David's been invited to go out on the salmon fishery this weekend with the *Julie II*. They're going tomorrow night for the Friday opening, and they'll be back Sunday morning. I didn't know whether you would let him go or not.'

'I don't know, Lucy. What about you? I know these openings. Sometimes the fisheries opens the season, then cancels the opening. He might be gone the three days, or he might only be gone one day. You'd have to stay at the boat by yourself, in case they came back early, in the middle of the night. How do you feel about staying alone down there at night?'

'I don't mind, Max. It wouldn't be the first

time. You've got a radio-telephone on board. And I'm sure I'm safer at night down there among the other live-aboards than I would be anywhere else in town at night.' Wharf life held no fears for her; it was what she knew best.

'Sorry, I'm forgetting your own childhood.' His laugh was low over the phone line. 'I guess you would be comfortable down there. I don't mind if David goes on the trip. They're good people, and it would be good experience for him. But don't let him go unless you feel okay about it yourself, Lucy. It bothers me that you'll be all alone at night.'

'That's ridiculous, Max!' Cheryl looked in, but Lucy waved her away, holding up five fingers to show how long she would be. 'I'm alone every night.'

'You shouldn't be,' he retorted. 'It's a state of affairs I mean to change.'

She swallowed past something painful in her throat. 'Max——'

'Do you miss me, Lucy?'

'Max, it's just not——' Her words trailed off.

'God, I miss you, Lucy. I miss you like hell!' Background noises came in around Max's voice. 'I love you, Lucy. You know I love you.'

The trouble was, she did know it. Trying to ignore his love for her was the hardest thing she had ever done.

'Don't, Max,' her whispered protest found him across the miles.

It sounded like a loudspeaker announcement along with Max's voice. 'I do, Lucy,' he insisted gently. 'Take care, love. They're calling my flight. I'll see you by Sunday.'

CHAPTER TEN

DAVID was exhausted from his hike. Lucy picked him up and they drove back to the boat where he let her cook a dinner which he ate hungrily. He fell asleep in the saloon while she was cleaning up from the meal. She covered him and pulled the curtains to dim the lights. It was summer in northern Canada, and the daylight lasted longer than the day for a tired twelve-year-old boy.

She went for a walk in the twilight, talking to one or two of the fishermen she passed. They were working on their boats, carrying provisions down and generally getting ready for the coming fishing opening. Most of them remembered a time when salmon were so plentiful that the salmon season was open for commercial fishing for weeks at a time. No longer. In an attempt to preserve the salmon, the government had been severely restricting the season, opening small areas for brief periods of time, rarely more than a few days at a time.

When she saw Gerry's father on the *Julie II*, Lucy stopped to tell him that David could accompany them in their trip.

'Good! Gerry'll be happy—he gets restless. Tell David that if he wants, he can go with Gerry tomorrow to pick out a couple of movies for the trip. That'll amuse them when things get dull.' He nodded at her and hoisted a duffle bag on to his shoulder.

Times had certainly changed. Life on a boat was changing along with everything else. A fishing trip now involved renting some movies to take along and play on the portable video. So much for the image of the simple West Coast fisherman!

Lucy spent the next morning working with Max constantly in her mind. What was she going to do about him? He had become so entangled in her life, how could she escape him? There seemed no logical reason why she could not leave and put half the world between herself and Max. No reason, except that she didn't want to. She had things to do here, things to finish. She felt good about what she was creating in this relatively isolated part of the world, and she wanted to go on, to watch it grow and develop.

She stopped at her apartment on the way home, to pick up fresh clothes. David prowled the rooms curiously.

'Is this where you live? It doesn't look like your place at all.' He looked at the empty walls, the anonymous furniture.

'I haven't had much time to fix it up, get pictures and things.' Why was she apologising to a twelve-year-old child?

'I like our boat better,' he told her. 'It's nicer.'

Lucy looked around at the empty apartment.

'I like the boat better, too,' she agreed.

That night, with David aboard the *Julie II*, she waved at them as they pulled away from the dock. Standing alone in silence, she looked around at the other boats. The few fishing boats that were left were in the process of leaving, or getting ready to leave. The remainder were pleasure boats, with only a couple of live-aboards.

Wanderlust was empty; Lucy felt it as she boarded, with only the faint shadow of Max and David's ghosts to greet her. Sleep eluded her, and she tossed restlessly in Max's bed, finally giving up, piling the pillows up so she could sit in bed and read a book she found in Max's shelves.

Even the fast-moving thriller she found could not still her restlessness. She read the words slowly, meaninglessly, trying to force interest by an effort of will, till finally, frustrated, she gave up and turned out the light, tossing in the dark until she fell into a fitfull sleep. She spent the night pursued by tortuous dreams.

Friday morning dawned and she awoke, lying in the half light of the cabin. She was exhausted, as if she had not slept at all. Outside, the sun was gone. Rain again, as if the sun would never shine. Endless rain. She straightened the tumbled sheets and drank her coffee standing in the galley. Max would be back in two days. Max, wanting a commitment, wanting an answer to his proposals, both business and personal.

She wasn't ready to face Max yet.

She picked up her handbag and locked up the boat, the rain dripping on her neck from the boom of the mainsail above her as she turned the key. A dull day, depressing and empty. She worked her way through the hours, eating lunch alone in her office, thinking of relaxed lunches with David. She worked late, but accomplished little. Her mind wasn't operating at peak efficiency, or even half.

It was close to nine when she stopped working.

As she closed the outside door behind herself, two lovers dodged around her, holding hands, seeing only each other, Not young lovers; the woman was several years older than Lucy.

Not too late, Lucy.

Time you had a lover, Lucy. Time for love.

Max, haunting her. Max would be back on Sunday, two days away, wanting answers . . . commitments. What was she going to say? What kind of answers was she going to give him?

The overcast was breaking, touches of blue starting to show in the sky. Tomorrow might be a good day. She didn't know what she would do tomorrow. Saturday. Wait for Max . . . waiting.

She hadn't eaten all day, she wasn't hungry, but the weakness, the depression could well be from lack of food. Cooking seemed more effort than she could bother with, so she drove to Smiles.

It was a mistake. Couples, groups, were laughing and talking over the plain tables and the good food. She watched them dully from her own table, hearing Max's voice, too. She drank her coffee slowly, stretching out the time until the food came. She could hear Max calling her—always Max, calling to her. Not answering was taking its toll, exhausting her and leaving her empty. Staying away from *Wanderlust* was no answer, it seemed to make it worse.

The sun had set by the time she left the restaurant. It was twilight, fading fast, as she drove along the waterfront road. A crowd of women, dressed in gumboats, white overalls, and headscarfs, had just come off shift at the cannery. Lucy drove slowly and carefully to avoid the women walking on the narrow road. There was no pavement; it was the kind of road where one drove carefully, watching for pedestrians, watching for trains at the frequent crossings.

She parked in the parking lot at the Rushbrooke floats and walked to the ramp. Strange, coming back with David not here, Max away. The tide was at its lowest, the ramp down to the docks angled steeply. For days she had been telling herself she should keep flat sneakers in her car, but she had forgotten and had to negotiate the steep ramp in high heels once again.

With the fishing fleet out, the floats seemed so empty. The boats she passed were familiar now, and she speculated on them, wondering if the man who owned the rotting wooden cruiser planned to get to work on it soon, if the big seiner fishing boat was going to get used this summer—it had seemed unused and abandoned since she had first seen it.

Wanderlust was there, of course; she could see the masts as soon as she started down the ramp. There seemed to be a new arrival farther out; she could see the single aluminium mast just beyond *Wanderlust*'s two wooden masts.

It was going to be a long, lonely night. For years she had lived alone, now suddenly one lonely night seemed unbearable.

She had to do something, not give in to this depression. Max's yacht was like any other boat, there were always jobs to be done. He and David had just finished sanding and varnishing all the outside woodwork. Inside, *Wanderlust* was clean and well tended, too. But there were things to be done. The hatches in the galley that contained food and dishes were badly disorganised, and Lucy suspected that Max and David spent a lot of time searching for things that were improperly put away. She could spend the evening tearing apart the contents of those hatches, emptying them and reorganising them.

She felt the emptiness she expected as she boarded and unlocked the door, but forced herself to ignore the feeling. She would have to work hard to get all those hatches done tonight. She had no time for wallowing in depression. She lit the lanterns and raided Max's clothes cupboard for working clothes. The jeans she found were too big, so she rolled the legs up and found a short length of rope to use for a belt. The shirt she tied halter-style beneath her breasts. She hung her cotton suit on the hooks in Max's cabin.

She started with the upper row of hatches under the counter, then emptied the lower row. There was such a lack of organisation that she had to empty all the cupboards before she could think about putting things back. As she emptied, she organised things roughly around her—dishes on the counter, food on the table, pots and pans on the floor, and miscellaneous items like flashlights and stereo headphones wherever she could find a corner for them.

While she was unloading cupboards, she heard a large boat steam out, and *Wanderlust* rocked gently for a minute in the wake. The nightly jet roared overhead as it came in to land at nearby Digby Island airport. Lucy poured hot water and cleaner in a pail, then started washing out the empty hatches.

When someone stepped on to the boat, she felt the motion. A man, probably a nearby boater, come to borrow something. Casual borrowing of wrenches, screwdrivers and other minor tools was always common on the waterfront.

Lucy was surrounded by pots and pans, hemmed in by the mess of her clean-up project. If she got up she'd be tripping amid the clatter of cooking utensils.

'Come on in!' she shouted out.

He came in, stopped at the entrance to the galley, looking at her sitting crosslegged on the floor amid that colossal mess.

'Max!' she breathed.

He pushed aside some pots and moved into the galley.

'I was cleaning up.' She gestured to the chaos. She didn't think her legs would hold her if she tried to stand up. She remained sitting, the soapy cloth still in her hand.

'I see that.' A coffeepot clattered on to its side as he moved closer to her, then dropped down to sit beside her.

'You're early. You said Sunday.' Her voice sounded odd.

'Did you miss me?' He wasn't smiling, just watching her solemnly.

She realised she'd been smiling, grinning at him. She sobered.

'Yes, I did.' She had missed him. Empty, like the world dried up. The world without Max.

'I want to talk to you.' She couldn't remember seeing him so tense before.

'What?' She didn't want him to look so worried.

He took her hand, removed the cloth from it, then covered it with both of his. She watched him, frozen herself; she had no will to move her hand away.

'When you told me about Ted, your husband, I——' her hand hurt briefly as a spasm went through him, gripping her hard, 'I had trouble handling that, knowing how you'd been hurt—especially knowing that you were still tied to him. I couldn't bear the idea of another man having a claim on you—that you were still legally married to him. I——'

'Max,' she interrupted earnestly, 'I—I've been thinking about that lately—about my marriage to Ted.'

'And?' He watched her intently.

'I don't want to be Lucy Carter. It's time I faced up to Ted, asked him for a divorce. I've avoided it, didn't want to think about Ted or see him. It's time I did.'

'I saw him.' Max's eyes were still on her. It seemed he hadn't blinked.

Lucy didn't think she could have heard him properly.

'You saw Ted? When? Why?'

'Yesterday.' He turned her hand, examining her palm. 'Did you know you have a long life-line?'

'Where did you see him? Why? You flew to the States——'

'California,' he agreed. 'Los Angeles. He was easy to find—in the phone book. I thought he would take longer to find. He might have left California.'

Max had gone looking for Ted. She had told

him she was still married, and he had flown off almost immediately.

'That's why you left here?' He'd gone the next day.

'I had to go some time soon, to check on things at S.C.S. I've been flying back every two months, to keep up with what Chan is doing. I would have waited to leave, hoping to talk you into coming with me—but when you told me about your marriage, then I thought I'd better go right away.'

He let her hand loose and reached into his jacket breast pocket and he withdrew a long envelope. 'He gave me this. He said he could get another copy from his lawyer.'

'Lawyer?' queried Lucy.

Max handed her the envelope. She opened it and withdrew the papers within. A legal document—a final divorce decree.

'He divorced me—a year ago!' She didn't have to call Ted or write to him. She could have faced him, but she was glad she didn't have to.

'I think he felt guilty about you,' said Max. 'He said to give you his best wishes.'

'Oh.' Lucy stared at the paper in front of her. She was free, single. How odd that she had been free of him for a year and not known it.

'I told him that if he ever came near you again I would kill him,' said Max flatly.

'You probably scared the life out of him. He'd think you meant it.' Max had sounded deadly then—a dangerous man.

'I meant it.' She believed him. 'I told him you were marrying me.'

Wanderlust rocked gently against the float.

'Max——' He wasn't touching her now. If he touched her, she knew she would melt. Her bones would turn to rubber and her blood to liquid fire. She ached for his touch. 'I—I'm scared, Max.'

He didn't touch her. He stood up and pushed his hands deep into his trousers pockets. 'Lucy, I love you. I want you sharing my home and my life. I want to make love with you.' His eyes locked with hers. 'I think you know it could be good, you and I together. I would never hurt you, Lucy.'

The pot by her left foot went crashing noisily as she got up. Barefoot, she still had to look up to him. She wondered what it would feel like, making love with Max. She had no brassiere on under his shirt, and the buttons had come undone, leaving only the knot below her breasts. She felt his eyes on her cleavage, his awareness that she was naked beneath the shirt. His arousal excited her, made her breasts thrust out against the shirt.

'Max, I want you to make love to me,' she whispered, 'even though I'm nervous about it. But I don't know about the rest—about marriage.'

'I'm afraid to come near you,' he told her. 'All these bloody pots—I might break my leg!'

'Max, I mean it. I'm not ready to be married Maybe I never——'

'Let's take it one step at a time,' he urged gently. 'First, come here. You haven't kissed me hello.'

He was right. She had been lonely and miserable, and now Max was here. She moved towards him, somehow missing the jumble on the floor. She moved into his arms, feeling his hands on her back as he drew her towards him. She raised on to her toes to reach his cheek.

'Hello,' she whispered as she kissed his cheek.

'You can do better than that.' His hands rested gently on her, hardly moving.

'Yes,' she agreed. She moved her lips to his, moving softly against him. His lips were soft and still, waiting for her, and she teased them gently with her own, knowing suddenly that he was waiting for her to make the advance, to tell him she was ready. The feel of his wind-roughened lips on hers was very erotic.

She moved closer to him, reaching up to pull his face closer to her, tangling her fingers in his hair. Her breasts were crushed against his chest, her softer thighs pressed hard against his. She felt his masculine body respond to her, and a spasm passed through his body as he groaned her name, but his hands remained still on her back.

'Make love to me, Max,' she whispered, opening her lips to him. His hands tightened on her back, then found the sensitive skin of her bare midriff, and Lucy gasped as he trailed his fingers across the skin below her ribcage. Her fingers fought against the thick material of his suit jacket, wanting the feel of his skin against hers.

He drew away from her, taking her hand to lead her towards the back of the boat.

'I've been sleeping in your bed,' she warned him as they crouched to go through the passageway to the back cabin.

He drew her into his cabin, shrugged off his suit jacket and drew her into his arms. 'I imagined you sleeping here. I hoped you were here, wanting me.'

She moved away from him to sink down on to the bed, leaning against the pillows she had piled up to read. She reached out a hand to him, an invitation. She saw that her hand was shaking slightly, knew her breath was shallow and quick.

'Max, please——'

He was beside her, his hands gentle on her face. 'Don't worry, Lucy,' he whispered as his lips touched hers. He traced the lines of her face, stroked her curls back from her face. Her eyes closed and her lips moved under his, opening to his advances.

His kiss deepened and she opened herself to him. His lips on hers, probing sensuously, his hands exploring her neck and shoulders. When he lifted his lips from hers, she struggled to open her eyes, the dizziness of passion receding slightly, momentarily. She found her arms wrapped tightly around him, her head cradled by his arm.

His face was close, his expression softer than she had seen before. She loosened her arms to explore the breadth of his shoulders, the hardness of his chest. Her hands found the top button of his shirt and loosened it, and the next, so that she could tangle her fingers in the sparse growth of hair on his chest.

The hand that had traced the shape of her neck moved gently down, moving down the crevice between her breasts, where her earlier exertions had left the buttons open. His fingers brushed against the insides of her breasts, then moved to cup her left breast through the cotton fabric of his shirt. Through the fabric, he grasped the nipple of her breast gently, rubbing it between thumb and forefinger, sending waves of erotic sensation through Lucy's whole body.

She arched towards him, seeking the deepness of the intimate kiss he had broken off only a moment before, pushing his shirt aside so that she felt his warm dry skin against her bare midriff. His two hands cupped her breasts, tracing designs of passion on the sensitive skin through the cotton.

'Lucy, the sight of you in my clothes is very sexy,' he murmured, moving away from her lips to kiss the tip of one breast through the cotton fabric.

She moved her hands to undo the single knot that held the shirt in position over her breasts, to let his hands and lips roam at will over her upper body.

Max moved her hands away, kissing her arms, her neck, the exposed skin between her breasts. 'Not yet,' he whispered, moving against her, moving his hands and his mouth against her to inflame her until she was twisting in his arms, needing him closer, closer.

Lucy didn't know when he loosened the knot of the shirt, but she gasped with pleasure when his hands covered the naked skin of her breasts. She pushed his shirt down over his shoulders so that she could feel his arms and shoulders, trace across his chest, feeling the wiry, masculine hairs on her palms. He shrugged the shirt away so that it dropped on to the floor and she felt her body against his, her warm, soft skin heating from the contact with his nakedness.

When his mouth bent to her breast, she could not stop herself from groaning with pleasure. He teased the nipple with his tongue, holding her body as it twisted in response. His hands moved along her hips, rested there lightly until she began to writhe in passion, then he stroked her thighs, his touch seeming to penetrate the heavy denim of the jeans she wore as if it were silk.

He loosened the rope she had used as a belt, unfastened the button at the waist and slid down the zipper. When the front opening parted, he ran his fingers lightly over the silky fabric of her panties, causing her to writhe her body against his, to thrust against him, inflamed with the need to have her new-found woman's passions satisfied.

'You're driving me mad!' she gasped as he moved his hands away from her abdomen, back to her midriff.

'Good.' Max held her full breasts in his two hands, holding the aroused nipples up as he bent to each one and sucked gently. 'I want to drive you mad.'

When his hands slid down her body, she moved against him, lifting to help him undress her.

They lay together, with nothing but the air to separate them. Max gently moulded her body to his, teaching her the feel of him, inflaming her to greater heights so that she clutched at him, needing him to satisfy the fire burning deep in her, consuming her.

'I love you, Lucy.' He moved over her. Briefly, there was no touching between them, no contact, but her body cried silently its need for his. As he moved down towards her, she reached to draw him to her. He entered her, completing her. Lucy clutched him to her, spinning off, losing touch as he moved with age-old rhythm. Together, they climbed a spiral of desire. Their world was the all-encompassing thrusting demand of their bodies, touching, moving, stimulating each other to a madness, a height that seemed unbearable. Then, at the peak, their bodies and their souls in perfect communion, together they achieved the perfect release of true lovers.

There was no wind, no sound, no motion. The full moon outside illuminated the cabin with a gentle, half-light. Lucy had slept deeply and dreamlessly, yet it was still night, nowhere near morning. As she awoke she became aware of Max's arm lying over her hip, of her own body curled against his. She lay quietly and listened to his deep breathing. In sleep, his face was relaxed and vulnerable.

She slipped carefully out of the bed, picking up her clothes from the day before and dressing hurriedly but quietly. Before she left the cabin, she looked back at Max's sleeping form. A few hours ago he had shown her body a pleasure she had never known before, and her body had responded to his like a violin to its master. They had been two souls, perfectly mated.

Now she had to get away. After what had happened between the two of them, it would not be possible to maintain any sort of distance between herself and Max once he awoke, and right now, she needed distance.

Outside, the water shone with moon-bathed

brilliance, Lucy had come out barefoot, not wanting to wear high heels on the dock, and her bare feet made no noise on the wooden planks.

Because it was high tide, the ramp was only slightly sloped. She climbed it and walked out to the end of the wharf, away from the parking lot. This area was used only for loading and unloading boats using the crane. At this time of night it was deserted and would remain so.

She sat on the end of the wharf, dangling her feet over the side. Below her and in front of her, the floats stretched out, a complex network of vessels. From her bird's eye view she could see *Wanderlust*'s masts and part of the hull itself.

Max wanted her to marry him, to be his wife and mother to his son. To be in his bed every night. Last night her body had told her how much she could enjoy sharing his bed. From the first time he had touched her, back in Toronto, her body had known that Max was the perfect lover for her. But she had come West, running from that knowledge. She had been frightened by her vulnerability to Max, yet she had hardly imagined the extent of that vulnerability.

If she stayed, she could be hurt—badly hurt. Max had wound himself so deeply into her mind and her heart that she could hardly conceive of a life without him. When he had left for a few days, her world had become dark and dismal. She feared that every day, every minute she spent with him would increase her dependence on his love.

Of course she loved him. When he appeared, her world became brighter. Life with Max around had twice—no, ten times—the depth. If something were to happen to him——

She had a sudden horrifying vision of Max dead, killed in some terrible accident. If he were gone from her, if there were no chance of being with Max, then life would become a long series of days, hours, minutes, seconds . . . of emptiness. Without Max, how long would it take for life to stir within her again?

She would be crazy to walk away from him, give him up for a lifetime of empty apartments and empty professional achievements. Making her life with him, she ran the risk of being hurt by her own vulnerability to him. Making a life without him, she would doom herself to half a life, empty of love.

She hadn't thought of children before, but having a child with Max could be fun. Not yet; they had many things to do first. Or maybe——

It was time she went back. Max was sleeping. If he woke and saw her gone, he might think she had run from him again. He had pursued her across a continent the last time she ran.

He must have needed her badly, to search so far and so long.

She ran back, her bare feet slapping on the wood. She was breathless when she turned on to *Wanderlust*'s finger. She slowed and tried to catch her breath. *Wanderlust* was in darkness, but in his cabin, Max was awake.

'You're awake . . . in the dark.' It wasn't dark; she could see him plainly by the light of the moon.

'I was waiting, hoping you would come back.' He wasn't smiling. 'I prayed that you would come back.'

She saw his need of her in his eyes, knew then that he was as vulnerable as she was. Their openness, their vulnerability to each other was what made the depth of their love possible—what gave their love strength and durability.

'You know what I felt last night, Max. I had to get away for a while, to be sure that whatever I decided, it was a decision for ever, not just a decision of passion.'

She touched his face and he reached up to hold her hand against his skin.

'Passion?' he queried softly. He traced down her hand and forearm with his fingertips. 'Why do you think there is such passion between us?'

She clasped his hand to still it. 'Because I love you, and because——' she said what she knew was true, 'you love me.' She let his hand loose and placed her hands on his chest, felt the roughness of his curly hairs beneath her hands.

'You're going to marry me?'

'Yes,' she agreed. She let her hands wander lower, watched his eyes change. 'Any time you want.'

'It better be soon,' growled Max, pulling her down towards him. 'We'll get a licence on Monday. There'll probably be a waiting period.' He wasn't waiting, his hands were busy removing her clothes.

'Five days,' she told him. Where had she learned that? 'Five days in British Columbia.'

She bent to kiss his neck, his shoulder, lower . . . to discover that his male nipples were almost as sensitive as her own. His response to her advances inflamed her. Last night he had made love to her, holding himself in check, being gentle and patient of her nervousness. She gently mouthed his nipples, moving her hands over his chest, the hard muscles of his abdomen, knowing from the tightening of his hands on her that in a moment he would take the lead away from her.

Then, together, they would enter paradise again.

Later, when they were still and satisfied, their bodies lay together, curled as one.

'This time you're not going to disappear.' Max held her against him.

Lucy turned her head so that her cheek rested against his chest.

'David will be back on Sunday.'

'Until then, what do you think we should do with ourselves?' He moved against her suggestively.

'There's a mess in the galley we could clean up. What are you going to tell David?' Only moments ago she had been more completely satisfied than ever before in her life, yet Max's movements against her were arousing her again.

'I'll tell him he's invited to the wedding. Then after the wedding, he can fly back to his grandmother for the summer.'

'Won't he mind? What about your mother? Are you sure——'

'I saw her when I was in Toronto and told her I hoped to be married the next time she saw me. She said it was about time, and offered to take David for the summer. As for David, after our trip to Lucy Island he told me I should marry you before someone else got you.' His hands rubbed her back gently, finding erotic points on her body that she had never dreamed of. 'Would you like to spend the summer sailing? We can find a lot of places on this coast that are completely deserted—beautiful places.'

Lucy stirred against him. In a moment the talking would end for a time. 'First I have to do something about Dr Fletcher, and Princess Fishery. I'm in the middle of both.'

'Give them proposals, tell them work can start on their systems in September if they want to go ahead. We'll come back for the beginning of September, get David back and started in school here. Meanwhile——' Max cupped her breast in his hand, teasing it to deep arousal while his hand stroked her thigh.

'You have to help me with Dr Fletcher. Programming costs, length to implementation . . .'

'I thought you'd never ask! Flowcharts,' he bent his lips to hers, 'in my briefcase . . . Ontario system, only slightly different. Shouldn't take too much to get your doctor sorted out.' His words were muffled by his lips on her lips, on her neck, moving to her breast.

'Speaking of flowcharts——' Her words were buried by her gasp.

Later. Later she would tell him her idea for flowcharting on computer. He would like it.

. . . much later.

Hello!

You've come to the end of this story and we truly hope that you enjoyed it.

If you did (or even if you didn't!), have you ever thought that you might like to try writing a romance yourself?

You may not know it, but Mills & Boon are always looking for good new authors and we read every manuscript sent to us. Although we are proud to say that our standards are high and we can't promise every aspiring author success, unless you try you'll never know whether one of those new authors could be you!

Who knows, from being a reader you might become one of our well-loved authors, giving pleasure to thousands of readers around the world. In fact, many of our authors were originally keen Mills & Boon readers who thought, "I can do that" — and they did! So if you've got the love story of the century bubbling away inside your head, don't be shy: write to us for details today, sending a stamped addressed envelope. We'd really like to hear from you!

The Editors

Please write to: